Jacqueline Wilson

Midnight

Illustrated by Nick Sharratt

CORGI YEARLING BOOKS

MIDNIGHT
A CORGI YEARLING BOOK 0 440 86578 6

First published in Great Britain by Doubleday,
an imprint of Random House Children's Books

Doubleday edition published 2003
Corgi Yearling edition published 2004

3 5 7 9 10 8 6 4

Corgi Yearling Books are published by Random House Children's Books,
61–63 Uxbridge Road, London W5 5SA,
a division of The Random House Group Ltd,
in Australia by Random House Australia (Pty) Ltd,
20 Alfred Street, Milsons Point, Sydney, NSW 2061, Australia,
in New Zealand by Random House New Zealand Ltd,
18 Poland Road, Glenfield, Auckland 10, New Zealand,
and in South Africa by Random House (Pty) Ltd,
Endulini, 5A Jubilee Road, Parktown 2193, South Africa

THE RANDOM HOUSE GROUP Limited Reg. No. 954009
www.kidsatrandomhouse.co.uk

A CIP catalogue record for this book is available from the British Library.

Printed and bound in Great Britain by
Cox & Wyman Ltd, Reading, Berkshire.

Dear C.D.,

Mum and Dad are going out tonight to a big dinner and dance. I've never been to a dance unless you count school discos and they were awful. I thought Will might come and talk to me. I knew he wouldn't dance with me, though we used to do all sorts of crazy dance routines at home. But Will acts like he doesn't even know me at school. A lot of the time he acts like we're strangers at home too. It's ever since he found out. It's changed everything.

I wonder if you ever go to dances? I always look in the papers and the party pages of Mum's *Hello!* magazine just in case I might catch a glimpse of you. I did get hopeful when I read that *Midnight* won the Book of the Year Award at some glitzy publishing do. I went to WHSmith's after school for a week, thumbing through everything, hoping there might be a photo of you. I saw a woman with long blonde hair holding a copy of *Midnight* and a big gold trophy in the shape of a pen nib. Is she your wife? Your girlfriend? She's very pretty.
And very lucky.

With love from
Violet
XXX

Also available by Jacqueline Wilson

Published in Corgi Pups, for beginner readers:
THE DINOSAUR'S PACKED LUNCH
THE MONSTER STORY-TELLER

Published in Young Corgi, for newly confident readers:
LIZZIE ZIPMOUTH
SLEEPOVERS

Published in Doubleday/Corgi Yearling Books:
BAD GIRLS
THE BED & BREAKFAST STAR
BEST FRIENDS
BURIED ALIVE!
THE CAT MUMMY
CLIFFHANGER
THE DARE GAME
DOUBLE ACT
GLUBBSLYME
THE ILLUSTRATED MUM
THE LOTTIE PROJECT
THE MUM-MINDER
SECRETS
THE STORY OF TRACY BEAKER
THE SUITCASE KID
VICKY ANGEL
THE WORRY WEBSITE
THE JACQUELINE WILSON COLLECTION
includes THE STORY OF TRACY BEAKER *and*
THE BED AND BREAKFAST STAR
JACQUELINE WILSON'S DOUBLE-DECKER
includes BAD GIRLS *and* DOUBLE ACT
JACQUELINE WILSON'S SUPERSTARS
includes THE SUITCASE KID *and* THE LOTTIE PROJECT
THE JACQUELINE WILSON BISCUIT BARREL
includes BURIED ALIVE! *and* CLIFFHANGER

Published in Doubleday/Corgi books, for older readers:
GIRLS IN LOVE
GIRLS UNDER PRESSURE
GIRLS OUT LATE
GIRLS IN TEARS
DUSTBIN BABY
LOLA ROSE

For Trish

MIDNIGHT

Dear C.D,

Mum and Dad are going out tonight to a big dinner and dance. I've never been to a dance unless you count school discos and they were awful. I thought Will might come and talk to me. I knew he wouldn't dance with me, though we used to do all sorts of crazy dance routines at home. But Will acts like he doesn't even know me at school. A lot of the time he acts like we're strangers at home too. It's ever since he found out. It's changed everything.

I wonder if you ever go to dances? I always look in the papers and the party pages of Mum's *Hello!* magazine just in case I might catch a glimpse of you. I did get hopeful when I read that *Midnight* won the Book of the Year Award at some glitzy publishing do. I went to *WHSmith's* after school for a week, thumbing through everything, hoping there might be a photo of you. I saw a woman with long blonde hair holding a copy of *Midnight* and a big gold trophy in the shape of a pen nib. Is she your wife? Your girlfriend? She's very pretty.
And very lucky.

With love from
Violet
XXX

From *Elfin Folk* by Casper Dream

The Changeling Child
Fairies steal away beloved babies and leave a changeling child
in their place. These base elfin breeds are often evil,
with difficult, demanding natures and enormous appetites.

One

'Are you sure you're going to be all right?' Mum asked.

'They'll be fine,' said Dad. 'Come on, or that mini-cab chap will start creating.'

'You've got the number of the hotel just in case?' said Mum. 'It's by the phone. Of course, in a *real* emergency you'd better call the police.'

'There wouldn't be much point. They'll all be at your dance,' I said.

Dad bared his teeth in a silly smile. He'd swapped his dark tunic and trousers and white working shirt for this equally naff evening uniform of satin-striped suit and frilly shirt. He wore a clip-on bow instead of his clip-on tie. And a clip-on face, pink, jovial, jowly, always Mr Plod the Policeman.

'Come on, Iris, quit flapping.'

'We should have driven them over to your mum's—'
She stopped and drew in her breath. We all knew we
couldn't go back to Grandma's.

'We should have got a babysitter,' Mum said lamely.

'We're not babies, Mum,' I said.

She gave me a quick kiss. She smelled weirdly sultry
after spraying herself liberally with last holiday's duty-
free Giorgio. Mum is so not a Giorgio girl, though she'd
tried hard tonight, wearing a Wonderbra to give herself an
impressive cleavage in her black clingy dress. It was a bit
too clingy. You could see the outline of her knickers as she
went to the living-room door. My mum would die rather
than wear a thong.

Still, who am I to talk? I wear little-girly white cotton
underwear and Mum would have me wearing little white
socks too if she could have her way. She treats me like I'm
three, not thirteen.

'Will? Come downstairs, we're going now,' Mum
called.

Will is fifteen, nearly sixteen. He's my brother. He's
not *just* my brother. He's always been my best friend too
– and my worst enemy.

I gave him my first smile when I was six weeks old.
When I was six months I'd hold out my arms to him,
straining for him to pick me up. I can't remember, of
course. These are Mum's little stories, but she always
tells the truth. Well. That's what we thought.

I can remember way back though, when I was still in
my buggy. Will would kneel in front of me and give
me my own private puppet show. A fairy story. I was

4

Goldilocks, even though my hair was black, and there were just two bears, not three. Big Growl, Will's bear, and Little Growl, my bear.

Will wasn't even at school yet but he made up plays that lasted for hours. No, not *hours* – and they can't have been real plays. He just made Big and Little Growl dance about in front of me, one of them booming in a glorious great growl, one of them squeaking in a winsome weeny growl. I know that's all it can have been, and yet the carpet around me sprouted forests and Big Growl and Little Growl padded about me on real paws. I reached out and patted their furry bodies and smelled the honey on their breath.

When Will started school Mum tried to play Teddies with me, a trite game of 'This is Big Growl and this is Little Growl'. They stayed shabby toys, their glass eyes glazed, their mouths stitched. But the moment Will was back they would lift their snouts in the air and growl a welcome. It was obvious. Will was magic.

He could work black as well as white magic even when we were both very young.

'You wait, Vi,' he'd say, if he thought I'd pinched the biggest cake at tea time or had one turn too many on our shared swing.

The waiting was the worst. He always knew how to bide his time. He'd generally wait until we'd both been put to bed. Then he'd creep into my room.

'Big Growl's very angry with you,' he'd whisper in my ear. 'He's going to bite your nose right off.' Will would pinch my nose hard. 'He's going to rip you into

5

ribbons with his claws.' Will would scratch down my arms, his nails digging right in. 'He's going to smother you with his great big bum.' Will would shove Big Growl onto my face, pressing harder and harder.

I got my head free and screamed once. Mum came running into my room.

'Oh, poor Violet's having a nightmare. I've given her Big Growl to cuddle,' said Will, without missing a beat.

I could have shown Mum my scarlet nose or my scratches but I didn't dare. She never suspected a thing.

Dad often looked at Will sideways, but then it was his job to be suspicious. And he didn't like Will even then. We all knew that for a fact, though no one said a word about it.

We don't talk about a lot of things.

Will barely talked to any of us now. He came home from school, fixed himself a gigantic sandwich and then sloped up the stairs to his bedroom. And stayed there. All evening. Mum used to take his supper on a tray but Dad said why should she act like a servant to her son? He expects her to act like a servant to *him*, but that's a different story. So now Will waits until he knows they're watching *News at Ten* and then sneaks down to the kitchen and heats himself a family-sized pizza or a whole pack of oven chips.

I've tried hanging out with him in the kitchen but he won't talk to me either. He'll grunt yes or no to any question but now he'll never initiate any conversation.

I can't bear it. I tried reaching out and taking his hand one time. He didn't snatch it away. He just looked down at our clasped hands as if they didn't belong to us. My hand went limp like a dead fish and I slithered it out of his grasp.

'Will!' Mum shouted now. 'Will, please come downstairs.' She was almost begging.

I thought he'd stay up in his room but his footsteps sounded on the stairs. Slowly, taking his time. But he came right down into the hall, through into the living room.

'Ah, there you are,' said Mum brightly. 'Now, you will look after your sister, won't you?'

Will stared at her silently. He'd changed out of his school uniform into a big grey shirt, soft black waistcoat, jeans and bare feet. He wore a string of little silver beads around his neck. His black hair stuck out oddly, as if he'd been running his hands through it. He looked even paler than usual, an almost greenish tinge to his white skin.

Half the girls at school are in love with Will. And some of the boys.

'Oh, we're going in for necklaces now, are we?' said Dad.

Will didn't blink. He went on looking at Mum.

'They're all the fashion for boys now,' she said quickly. 'Will? You're the man of the house tonight, all right? You're in charge.'

'OK,' said Will.

Mum's hitched-up chest heaved with relief. She smiled at Will. 'You'll look after Violet?'

'Sure,' said Will. 'Don't you worry, we'll be fine.'

'That's my boy,' said Mum.

She used to say that all the time to Will. She hadn't said it for ages now. Will waited until Mum and Dad were at the front door.

'I'm not your boy,' he said.

He spoke quietly but I know she heard. There was a long pause. Then Mum called another goodbye, sounding so forlorn.

'Goodbye, Mum,' I called, feeling sorry for her.

'Goodbye, Violet. Goodbye, Will. Goodbye, darlings.'

'For God's sake, you're starting to sound like the Walton family,' said Dad. 'Bye kids. Get to bed at a reasonable time. No larking about and staying up till midnight. We won't be back till very late. The dance doesn't end till one and then I expect there'll be a bit of faffing about chatting.'

'Yeah, you and your mates cracking open yet another bottle or two of whisky,' Will said softly.

They were out of the door by this time. Mum cried one more goodbye like some sad calling bird with only one song. Then the front door slammed shut.

We were on our own. I looked at Will. He looked at me, his deep-green eyes very bright. I thought he'd slope straight past me up to his room but he stayed where he was, staring at me. I tried to stare back but my eyes swivelled first. I looked foolishly round our boring beige living room and then looked back. Will was still staring.

'What?' I said, my heart thudding.

'I'm just subjugating you to my will,' he said.

'Shut up!' I said, giggling.

'No, you shut up, little Violet. I'm in charge, remember?' Will walked over to the brown corduroy sofa. Mum's side was neat, with her Maeve Binchy book and the *Radio Times* and several magazines carefully stacked beside her cushion. Dad's side was shiny, the seat dented with the weight of his fat bum. Will's lip curled.

'I'm so glad he's not my dad,' he said.

'Will, I'm so sorry. All that stuff Grandma said. She's mad. And stupid. How could Mum and Dad have kept it from you? They're mad too.'

'You don't get it, do you? It's wonderful. The biggest kick ever. I'm not part of this crappy family.'

'Yes you are. You're still my brother.'

'No I'm not, dozy.' He took hold of my wrist, twisting it to see the veins. He held his own wrist up too. His veins were much nearer the surface, delicate and very blue. 'Different blood.'

'Blue blood.'

'*Bad* blood.'

'I hate Grandma.'

'I love the daft old bag for turning my life around. I'll just hang out here till I'm eighteen and then I'm off.'

'To trace your real mother?'

'Well, she doesn't sound a bundle of laughs, does she? Some sad junkie who gave up her own kid? No thanks. I don't want any more parents. I'll be fine just by myself.'

'You won't be by yourself,' I said. 'Because I'll follow you and stick to you like glue.'

Will looked at me and then laughed. 'Right, little Miss Pritt. OK, let's eat.'

'Together?'

'Well, you can take yours down the road and round the corner but I'm sitting right here.' Will sat in Mum's chair, one leg straddling an arm.

'Mum's taken some of her fish pie thing out the freezer. And there's veg and stuff. I'll go and fix it, shall I?'

'We don't want that muck. We'll have pizza,' said Will.

'I don't think there's any left.'

'Take out!' He picked up the phone and ordered a giant Pizza Palace special with all the toppings, two portions of garlic bread, two large Cokes and a big carton of ice cream, chocolate, strawberry and vanilla.

I stared at him. I knew he didn't have any cash at all. Dad hadn't given him any pocket money for weeks and he'd confiscated his building society book. I tried to calculate how much I had in my purse. Less than a fiver. I had a pound or so in loose change rattling round in my school bag, but that was all.

'Credit card number? Sure,' said Will, and he reeled off a number and an expiry date. He put the phone down, grinning. 'Supper in twenty minutes, Violet.'

'Did you just make the numbers up?'

'No, they're Dad's. He left his wallet lying on the kitchen table. It was stuffed with twenty-pound notes, but knowing him, he'd have them all counted – and probably coated with PC Plod secret marking ink too.

10

Nicking his credit card was too obvious. Memorizing the number was a doddle.'

'But he'll find out later when he gets his statement.'

'In a month or more. Like who cares about the future? Let's live for now, Violet.'

So we shared the giant pizza and ate the garlic bread and drank the Cokes and spooned up every scrap of ice cream.

'You can have all the strawberry,' said Will, knowing it's my favourite.

It was wonderful being *us* again. I lay back on the sofa, totally full, blissfully happy.

'My tummy!' I said, rubbing it. 'It feels like it's going to burst.'

'You look like Muffy,' said Will.

She'd been his pet chinchilla. He'd had her for five years and loved her more than anyone. He'd never cuddle any of us, not even Mum or me, but he'd sit for hours with Muffy curled on his lap. Will rarely confined her to her cage. She had a habit of burrowing beneath a cushion or under the bed so you could never fling yourself down anywhere in case you squashed her. Will insisted she was fully house-trained but Muffy still had many accidents. I tried not to make a fuss when I sat on her small hard droppings.

I think Will was probably devastated when she died but we had started to keep to our own bedrooms and I had no way of telling. Mum and Dad had told us that we had to keep apart.

'Will's getting a big boy now. You don't want

to go running into his bedroom all the time,' said Mum.

'Yes I do!'

'Well, it's not sensible. He needs his privacy. And you need yours. Do you understand?'

They couldn't have really stopped us, but Will did start to want time by himself. He frequently yelled at me to get lost when I trailed after him. I felt so lonely without him.

'Will, why don't you get another chinchilla? Or some other kind of pet?'

'I don't want anyone else, thanks.'

'So have you still got Muffy's cage in your room?'

'Yep.'

'It must look a bit weird, empty.'

'You're the one with the weird bedroom. All those fairies flitting about. Have you still got them all hanging down from the ceiling?'

'Of *course* I've still got them,' I said.

'There's the Crow Fairy, the Dragonfly, the Rose – what else?'

'You can't have forgotten them! You used to play with them too! Come on, I'll remind you.' I pulled at Will's arm, and he followed me upstairs to my bedroom.

He walked in and smiled. 'Oh yeah,' he said, looking up at the fourteen fairies suspended from the ceiling. He reached up and gently flicked the Moonbeam Fairy so that she wavered, feathery wings wafting as if she was really flying.

She was my first successful fairy. I'd tried copying Casper Dream's illustration right from when I got my

12

first fairy book, but my funny little felt creations looked nothing like his beautiful artwork. They were too fat and lumpy, with button eyes and wool hair.

Then Miss Lang, the old lady who lived next door, taught me how to sew properly, showing me all the different stitches. She gave me a special sewing kit for Christmas, a little rag doll with a matching outfit of clothes. I wasn't very interested in making a rag doll but I used the basic pattern to fashion my own fairy. I pored over the picture of the Moonbeam Fairy in my book, doing my best to copy her properly.

I made her out of white silk, though it was very slippery to work with, and I sewed little pearls all round the hem of her dress. I gave her cream feathery wings and long white curly cotton hair way past her knees. She didn't look *exactly* like the Casper Dream illustration but she was much better than her lumpy felt fairy sisters.

Will liked my Moonbeam Fairy – and the Rose and the Bluebell and the Autumn Leaf fairy. He particularly liked the Crow Fairy. She crouched on the back of a black crow. I hoped it wasn't a real stuffed crow. I'd found it on an old hat in a junk shop. It seemed a simple replica, but there was something frighteningly real about its sharp orange beak and beady black eyes. I was never too sure about the Crow Fairy, especially when Will made her sweep through the air, casting evil spells.

He used to play all sorts of magical games with me and my fairies until Dad caught us at it.

'A lad of your age playing with *fairies*?' said Dad, his lip curling.

13

Will hadn't gone near them since. But now he reached up and touched them all, making them dance up and down on their elastic threads. He pulled the Crow Fairy by her tiny black toes so that she and her crow bounced up and down as if they were bungee jumping.

'Don't, Will.'

He took no notice. He pulled the other fairies in quick succession as if he was bell-ringing. Their wings flapped dementedly as the elastic pinged.

'Stop it!' I said, pushing him.

I pushed harder than I meant to. He lost his balance. He tripped, still hanging onto the Crow Fairy. Her elastic snapped and she flew across the room and landed in the corner, slipping right off her crow, breaking one of her feathery wings.

'Now look what you've done!' I said, kneeling down and examining her. 'Oh no, you've ripped her dress, look, and I haven't got any more black lace.'

'It was your fault, shoving me like that, you stupid girl,' said Will, but he knelt down beside me. He cradled the Crow Fairy and her bird in his hands. Her flimsy net dress had caught on the crow's sharp beak and had ripped beyond repair. Will poked his finger through the hole.

'Poor little ruined Crow Fairy,' he said. He flew the crow through the air, aiming it straight at me. 'Vicious beast. Watch out, Vi, it'll peck you to death.'

Will saw I wasn't in the mood for fooling around. He stopped larking, pulled a feather out of the crow's wing and stuck it into the Crow Fairy's soft back.

'There. She can fly again now. And you can make her a new dress, can't you? Haven't you got anything black? Look, I've got black socks, you can have them.'

'You don't put fairies in black wool. She'll look like she's in winter woollies, little cardie and mittens and bobble hat. It wouldn't work.'

'I know! My black velvet waistcoat,' said Will.

It was another junk shop find, a hippy-type waistcoat straight from the seventies, but it somehow looked amazingly cool on Will. It was his all-time favourite garment.

'We can't use your special waistcoat!'

'Sure we can,' said Will, taking it off. He thrust it at me. 'There. Get snipping.'

'I can't spoil your waistcoat.'

Will snatched the scissors out of my sewing box and cut right up the back of the waistcoat. 'There. I've spoilt it for you. Now get sewing. Have you got any black sequins? Black ribbon?'

I started cutting out a tiny black dress for the Crow Fairy. Will sat cross-legged beside me, watching. He dug in my sewing basket and found another pair of scissors. He started cutting something out himself from the ruined waistcoat.

'Are you going to sew, Will?'

'Boys don't *sew*,' he said, imitating Dad's voice so accurately I had to check his lips.

He went on cutting out a long soft strand of velvet with an hour-glass shape in the middle.

'What's that you're making? It won't fit her.'

15

'It's not for your little Crow Fairy. This is for you,' said Will.

He tied the shaped part over my eyes and knotted it behind my head. 'You too shall go to the masked ball, Cinderella,' he said.

'What are you now, a fairy godmother?' I said, pretending we were still larking about, though my heart was pounding.

I knew what was coming now.

Dear C.D,

Are you ever frightened?

Did you ever play games when you were young — really scary games?

There's a page in your Midnight book that really haunts me. At first glance it looks as if it's a completely black illustration, glossy and opaque. But then you see these eyes gleaming in the dark, amber and orange and green, and if you look very carefully you can see these strange twisted shapes. They could just be gnarled old trees — or they could be creatures waiting to get you.

I can't look at that page without my heart thudding.

With love from
Violet
XXX

From *The Book of Flower Fairies* by Casper Dream

The Violet Fairy
A small shy fairy, purplish blue, easily trampled upon.

Two

Will and I had played the Mask Game for years. We started when we were very young. Will was maybe six, me four. Dad forced us to go to a children's Christmas party at the police social club. We both loathed these parties. Will didn't want to charge round playing football and fighting with the other boys. I was much too shy to compare party dresses and disco dance with the girls. We both disliked the conjuring clown. Will was simply bored, and I was such a little wimp I was frightened.

I *did* quite enjoy the old-fashioned party games after we'd eaten our fill of sausage rolls and crisps and ice cream. I was good at playing Statues even though I was one of the youngest, and I won a pink brush and comb and hairslide set in a game of Pass the Parcel.

The only game I didn't like was Blind Man's Buff. I hated the way some big policeman 'uncle' tied a sash too tightly round my eyes so that I couldn't even blink. I didn't like being spun round and round in the sudden dark. I hated stumbling about with outstretched hands while the other children rushed past me giggling.

I kept running this way and then that way, grabbing thin air again and again. Some of the boys started poking me in the back and trying to trip me. I tried to pull the mask off but the uncle said, 'Hey, no peeking!' and brushed my hands away.

I felt as if I was stuck in this awful whirling black world for ever. I started to cry behind the sash. Then my hands suddenly clasped strong skinny arms.

'You've caught me,' said Will. 'OK, it's my go now.'

He'd stood right in front of me and deliberately let himself be caught. But I didn't realize that then. I wasn't grateful enough. Another little girl suggested we go off into a corner and play hairdressers with my new brush and comb and hairslides. She was at least a year older than me and very pretty, with long fair curly hair. I was immensely flattered that she wanted to play with me.

I brushed and combed her long curls and then carefully clipped each pink sparkly slide into place, one above the other. They kept slipping sideways but I tried again and again, breathing heavily, until they were perfect. The curly girl fingered them complacently.

'Now it's your turn to be the hairdresser,' I said.

She didn't want to swap roles. She tried combing my

thick black hair but gave up almost immediately, saying there were too many tangles.

'Brush it first,' I suggested.

This seemed too much like hard work for her. She dabbed at my hair ineffectually and then flapped her hands, saying it was making her arm ache.

'I'm tired of playing hairdressers anyway,' she said, and wandered off.

I followed her anxiously.

'No, I'm going to play with the big girls now. You're too little,' she said, pulling away from me.

'But what about my hairslides?'

'They're mine now,' she said, and then she ran away.

I looked round for Will. The game of Blind Man's Buff was over. He was standing by himself, frowning.

I started worrying. 'Hello, Will,' I said. 'I don't like that girl with curly hair. She stole my hairslides. Will you get them back for me?'

'You gave them to her,' said Will.

'I didn't.'

'Yes you did. I saw. When you went off to play with her.'

'I didn't want to,' I lied. 'She made me. I'd much rather play with you, Will.'

'Well, I don't want to play with you,' said Will.

He walked away and left me too.

He didn't talk to me in the car going home. He didn't say a word when we were getting ready for bed. He didn't respond when I called out to him after we'd been tucked up. I crept into his room in the middle of the night and tried to get into his bed but he pushed me straight out onto the floor. I cried and begged him to make friends but he wouldn't.

He kept it up for days.

'*Please* play with me, Will,' I begged.

He looked at me, his green eyes glittering. 'You really want to play with me, do you?' he said.

'You know I do.'

'Any game I like?'

'Of course. You can choose.'

'Then I choose Blind Man's Buff.'

I was trapped. Will's version of Blind Man's Buff was far scarier than the party game. I always had to play the Blind Man. Will let me blunder around for ages until he allowed himself to be caught. But that wasn't the end. That was only the beginning. I wasn't allowed to take the mask off. I had to let Will spin me round again and lead me along, across rooms, up the stairs, down the stairs, and then he'd stop me still and make me guess where I was.

If I got it wrong I had to pay a forfeit. Once when I tore off the mask I found I was standing at the very edge of the stairs. One small step forwards and I'd have gone hurtling down to the bottom. But Will was holding me. He wouldn't let me go. I had to trust him. That was hard. I loved him so much but I didn't really trust him at all.

I didn't trust him now, with the black velvet blindfold over my eyes. I fingered it anxiously. Will's hands slapped mine.

'Stop that! You know you have to keep it on, Violet.'

I swallowed. 'We're too old for silly games of Blind Man's Buff, Will.'

'Perhaps we can make the rules a little more sophisticated then,' said Will.

'I don't want to play.'

'Don't be silly, you always want to play with me.'

'Not Blind Man's Buff.'

'But it's our favourite game. And don't forget, I'm in charge tonight, Violet. You must do as I say.'

'Oh yeah, like you're my master and I'm your slave,' I said.

'Exactly,' said Will. He took hold of me by my wrist. He didn't hurt but he held me tightly enough to remind me of painful Chinese burns in the past.

Will pulled on my arm and I moved obediently. I still hated the obliterating sensation of the blindfold. It was as if the real world didn't exist any more because I couldn't see it. I didn't feel *I* existed either. It felt like my eyes had disappeared behind the black velvet.

Will led me across the living room. I responded to the slightest change of pressure of his finger, circum-navigating the table, the chairs, the edge of the bookcase. We walked through the doorway and into the hall.

I started to relax a little. It wasn't so bad. It was just a silly game. When I was small I panicked the moment I couldn't see, losing all sense of direction, all common sense. It felt as if Will was leading me through an endless labyrinth to some dark centre of the world.

But I could work out where he was taking me now. I

expected him to play the stairs trick again. I moved slowly and cautiously, keeping track. I wouldn't have to pay any humiliating forfeit. Maybe this time I was going to win.

We didn't go up the stairs. We went down the hall. I stumbled over something soft, like a small cat, but I worked it out in an instant. I wasn't going to let one of Mum's furry slippers faze me!

We went into the kitchen. I tried not to collide with the breakfast bar, the fridge, the waste bin in the corner. Will led me right across the room. I wondered if we were heading for the larder. Was Will going to try to cram me inside, under the bottom shelf? Oh God, he wasn't going to shut the door on me, was he? Then I'd still be in total darkness even if I tore the blindfold off.

'Will?'

'Shh! You can't concentrate if you talk. You're going to have to tell me where you are soon.'

'I know where I am. In the kitchen. Will, don't put me in the larder. I'll scream if you do.'

'And who would hear you? But don't underestimate me, Violet. I'm not doing anything as *obvious*. And how could even a skinny little squit like you *fit* in the larder? I'd have to chop you up first, jointing you just like a butcher.' He chopped at my body, using the flat of his hand.

'Stop it! You're hurting!'

'I'm barely touching you. You're such a little wimp. You're nearly *crying*.'

'No I'm not.'

24

'You're ever so scared though, aren't you?'

'Not the slightest bit,' I lied.

'Then why is your hand all cold and clammy?' Will said, clasping it suddenly. 'Yuck, jellyfish hands.' He let go and I heard him wiping his own hands unnecessarily on his jeans.

He let go.

I made a dash across the kitchen, trying to yank the blindfold off, but he'd tied it too tightly in a complicated knot. He caught me at once.

'Aha! You don't get away that easily.' He was camping it up, speaking in a silly sibilant stage-villain accent, but his fingers dug hard into my wrist, his nails hurting me. I had to let him lead me back across the kitchen. I tensed as we passed the larder but he didn't pause. I heard him turning a key, and then opening the back door.

Oh God.

He led me out into the garden, jerking me impatiently when I stumbled on the doorstep. I started shivering. It was too cold to be out without a coat.

'Are we going to be out here long, Will? Can I get a jacket? It's freezing.'

'Stop whining.' He pulled my arm and I had to follow.

It was much harder keeping a sense of where I was going. Especially as Will seemed to be walking us round in a circle.

'Round and round the garden, like a teddy bear,' Will said, reciting the baby's rhyme. 'One step. Two step. And a tickly under there.' His bony fingers scrabbled under my chin, scuttling down my neck.

'Stop it!'

'I'm not going to stop. We've only just started.'

I was getting hopelessly disorientated, not sure now if I was at the top or bottom of the garden. I wondered what forfeits Will would concoct. They used to be childishly disgusting. I had to eat a worm or lick snot. The worst time was having to drink ten glasses of water just before I went to bed, with inevitable consequences.

He wouldn't inflict these sorts of forfeits on me now, when we were practically grown up.

He'd think of worse ones.

He suddenly pushed me right into the hedge.

'For God's sake, Will!'

'Go on. Move. Push, Violet.'

Twigs tore at me, scratching my arms.

'What are you playing at, Will? You're hurting! Please let's stop.'

'Just shut up. You'll be through in a minute.'

He gave me one last shove and the threadbare hedge gave way. I was in the garden next door. Miss Lang's garden – only she didn't live there any more. Nobody did.

I'd always been a little scared of Miss Lang. She was very old, and she walked with a bad limp, so she had to use a black shiny stick. I didn't like the sound of its *tap tap tap*. I used to run away when I heard her coming, but one day she called after me and asked if I'd like to come to tea. I didn't fancy the idea at all but didn't know how to say no politely. It was a bit of an ordeal. I had to sit up straight and sip my tea very carefully from a golden cup and nibble daintily at pink wafer biscuits but I managed not to spill anything and Miss Lang seemed to take a shine to me. She asked Will to tea too, but he fidgeted and yawned and showered sponge cake crumbs everywhere and didn't get invited back.

I went to tea with Miss Lang on a weekly basis. In the summer we had tea in the garden. She made lemonade and iced fairy cakes and we ate them sitting in green canvas chairs under her apple tree. We'd chat for a little while and then Miss Lang would read me strange fairy stories from old-fashioned books with brightly coloured covers, yellow and red and blue and pink – and violet! She gave me *The Violet Fairy Book* for my tenth birthday, wrapping it up in rainbow paper and tying it with a purple satin ribbon.

Poor Miss Lang had a stroke soon afterwards and was taken away in an ambulance. She never came back. She didn't die straight away. Mum thought she'd gone into some kind of nursing home. Then a van came and someone cleared all the contents of her house, even the coloured fairy books. The house started crumbling and the garden became a thicket of brambles and ivy, as if the fairies in the books had put a spell on it.

Mum and Dad were forever complaining about the state of the house and the garden, saying it was dragging the price of *our* house down. Squatters moved in and held loud parties and Dad was outraged. He got them evicted eventually and after that the house was boarded up and the windows bricked in. It made it look ugly and frightening. The garden turned into a total wilderness, rank with weeds. Dad hacked savagely at any plant daring to creep over our fence.

Now I was standing in the garden, hunched up tight, not daring to take a step further. Will gripped my wrist tightly, tense himself. I wondered what he could see.

'Let's go back, Will,' I begged.

'No, Violet. Let's go forward,' said Will, pulling me.

The grass reached right up my legs so I had to wade through it like water. Brambles tore at me, branches flipped into my face. Will steered me slowly, telling me to duck and dodge, but I was clumsy with fear and kept blundering into things. I couldn't help thinking there might be someone in the garden watching us.

'Is there anyone there, Will?' I whispered.

'Oh yeah, Miss Lang's ghost. Watch out, she's coming to spook you,' said Will. 'Help, help, she's coming!'

I knew he was fooling around but I could suddenly see her, luminous white in a long nightgown, her face twisted sideways with her stroke. I could hear the rasp of her breath, the shuffle of her slippered feet, the *tap, tap tap* of her stick. I knew I couldn't see anything under my blindfold, and I was simply hearing my own breath, my own footsteps – but I still clutched Will desperately.

'Leave go of me!'

'But I'm so scared, Will. I hate it out here.'

'OK, OK. We'll go indoors,' said Will.

He didn't lead me back towards the gap in the hedge. He led me onwards, to the back of Miss Lang's house. He had to be playing another trick on me. We couldn't possibly get inside. All the doors were boarded up, the windows bricked in.

The windows at the front. They hadn't bothered to brick the back windows. I heard Will bashing at some catch and then felt him pushing hard. Something splintered and Will hurtled forwards.

'Now comes the tricky bit,' said Will, breathing heavily. 'You've got to do exactly as I say, Violet. Just follow me.'

I didn't *have* to follow him. I could tear the blindfold from my face and run away from him. I could barricade myself back in my own room till Mum and Dad came back. What was the time? What if they came home early and we were missing?

I couldn't concentrate on Mum and Dad now. This was just Will and me. I had to stand up to him. I wasn't a stupid baby any more. I didn't have to do what he said. He didn't have any real power over me. He still had a hold on me but he was scrabbling upwards, obviously trying to get in the window. I could tug my arm free now, when he was trying to balance on the sill. Now!

'Now, Violet!' Will hissed.

I did as I was told. I scrambled after him, blindly obedient. He hauled me up and swivelled me round and pushed me out over the sink. I got painfully caught on the taps for a moment but then I fell with a thump onto the cold kitchen floor.

I lay there, winded.

'Violet? Vi, are you all right?' Will touched my shoulder, giving me a little shake. He sounded scared but he still didn't take the blindfold off. I lay holding my breath as long as I could, wanting to make him really worried.

'I know you're pretending,' said Will, but he bent right down and put his face against mine to see if I was breathing. His cheek was as smooth and soft as a girl's. His hair tickled my forehead. I twitched.

'You bad girl,' said Will. He tickled me under the chin. I shrieked and squirmed away from him.

'There! Making out you're dead!'

'I *feel* dead,' I said. 'You're killing me, Will, dragging me into hedges and through windows, acting like we're on some crazy quest.'

'We're not finished, yet,' said Will.

'*Please* take the blindfold off. It's really hurting, cutting right into my head. My eyes feel like they're being poked back into my brain.'

I remembered my old baby doll and the terrible day her blue eyes disappeared into the back of her head and rattled inside. I felt as blind and helpless now.

Will pulled me along and I stumbled after him, through the kitchen, along the hall, in and out of the front room and then the living room. Our footsteps echoed horribly as we walked over the bare floorboards. I struggled to keep a plan of the house in my head but it was getting harder and harder. It stopped being Miss Lang's ordinary suburban semi, the mirror image of ours. It was distorted into a dark maze and I felt as if I was never going to find my way out.

Will led me up the stairs. I tripped on every step. We

seemed to be going up and up and up – but when we reached the top at last it still wasn't over. We didn't go right or left along the landing. We were going up again.

'Here,' said Will, putting my hands on the rungs of a ladder.

'I can't! I *can't*, Will. Not blindfolded.'

'Yes you can. I'm just behind. Go on. Up. *Up!*'

I went up, Will pushing me every time I stopped. I started sobbing, my nose running. I hated Will for doing this to me. I hated myself for letting him.

He was reaching over my head, struggling to push the trapdoor open. We were going up into the attic. I felt my way up the last few rungs of the ladder, knowing that I could easily fall and break my neck.

'I've got you,' said Will, beside me now, hand under my elbow, helping me. I hauled myself up, right into the attic.

There was a strange smell, not just dust and mould. I straightened up cautiously. I heard Will switch on the light. And then there was a flapping and a rushing as little creatures flew at me, their wings beating in my face.

Dear C.D,

I wonder if you've got a brother? Did he ever scare you when you were young? Did you ever stand up to him?

I wish I knew how to stand up to Will.

I wish you were my brother. I wish you were my friend. I wish you could write to me.

With love from
Violet
XXX

From *The Smoky Fairy* by Casper Dream

So the Smoky Fairy and the Magic Dragon flew away . . .

Three

They were bats, flying all round me, flapping their weird black wings. I screamed and screamed, waving my hands wildly, trying to beat them away. Will helped me tear the blindfold off and let me escape down the ladder first. My shoes slid on the rungs and I scraped my shins. I ran along the landing, raking my long hair with my fingers, terrified one of the bats might be tangled up in it.

I hurtled down the stairs, along the hallway, blundering in the gloom even without the blindfold. I heaved myself up onto the draining board in the kitchen, edged out of the broken window, and then raced down the garden. I wove my way through the long grass, scared there were more little darting creatures hiding there. I found the gap in the hedge and burrowed my way through.

I straightened up in our own garden. It looked so neat and ordinary, the grass clipped, all the plants carefully pruned. I ran to the back door and got into the kitchen just as the old grandfather clock in the hall was chiming midnight.

It was a shock seeing how muddy I was. I'd made dirty footprints across Mum's newly polished floor-tiles. I took my trainers off and rushed upstairs to the bathroom. I locked the door and then started running a bath, struggling out of my filthy clothes.

Will banged on the door. 'Vi?'

'Go away, you *pig*.'

'Oh, for God's sake, Violet.'

'I'm having a *bath*. Clear off.'

'Look, I didn't know about the bats, I swear I didn't.'

Will was so good at lying you never knew when he was telling the truth.

'Vi, talk to me.'

I pressed my lips together, rubbing soap all over myself. I dunked my head in the water too, massaging shampoo in so fiercely I scratched my scalp. I needed to wash away the feel of the bats. I kept twitching and shuddering as if they were still flying into my face.

'You're being very childish,' said Will, rattling the doorknob.

I said nothing, rinsing my hair.

'If you don't answer I'm coming in,' said Will.

My heart started thumping. I'd locked the door, but the lock was old and faulty. We both knew Will only had to shove the door hard and the lock would give.

I waited.

He waited.

Eventually I heard him walking away, along the landing to his own room.

I breathed out. The blood was beating in my head. I could even feel it in my eyelids. It felt as if tiny wings were trying to fly through my lashes. I rubbed my eyes hard with the towel, and then stood up. The bath had been too hot. I felt dizzy and had to lean against the wet tiled wall. When the room stopped whirling round I wrapped myself in the largest towel, grabbed my muddy clothes and listened at the door. I waited, steeling myself, and then made a dash for it along the landing to my own room.

I was in bed when Will came knocking again.

'Violet?'

I didn't have a lock, faulty or otherwise, on my bedroom door.

Will knocked again – and then opened the door.

'Get out!'

'I'm not *in*. Vi, please, I want you to listen to me. I didn't mean to frighten you. I just wanted to play the old game and I got a bit carried away. I was just trying to spook things up a bit by going next door. But then it got way too spooky, even for me. Those bats gave me a fright too. Did you see their little vampire faces and those pointy teeth? I didn't know they were lurking there, I swear I didn't. You do believe me, don't you?'

I picked up one of my early Casper Dream fairy books

and started slowly turning the pages, taking no notice of Will.

'Vi? Listen to me.'

He walked into the room and snatched my book away. I made a grab for it. Will held it high above his head.

'Give it back! Are you mad? It's a first edition, worth a fortune.'

'I'm not harming it.'

'Yes you are. You're getting your muddy hands all over the cover, look!'

Will looked, and saw the little smears from his fingerprints. He wiped the laminated cover with his sleeve.

'Gone,' he said, but he handed the book back, laying it down carefully beside me on the bed.

'You're crazy,' I said, opening the book again.

Will pulled a crazy face, eyes crossed, tongue lolling, nid-nodding his head in front of me.

I always found it weirdly frightening when he pulled faces. It was as if he'd really turned into someone else. I tried to take no notice, concentrating on the fairies in the book. Will started making mad gibbering noises, capering round my bed.

'Now who's being childish,' I said. 'And there's mud all over your shoes. Take them off. Go and have a bath. They'll be back soon.'

'Don't be daft. The old man will be out half the night getting sozzled,' said Will – but as he spoke we heard the car draw up outside.

'Oh cripes,' said Will, losing all his cool.

He pretended he couldn't care less about Dad

but he was still a bit scared of him. We all were.

'Quick!' I hissed. 'Get into your bed with your clothes on. Pull the duvet right up so Mum won't see. Oh help, wait!' I sat up and wiped a muddy smudge from Will's cheek.

I was still mad at him but it was always Will-and-me against the parents, no matter what.

'Thanks, Vi,' Will whispered, and then he ran off to his own room.

I hoped he wasn't making any more muddy footprints. The landing light was off so maybe they wouldn't show. I switched my own moon-globe bedside lamp off and lay in the dark, listening. I heard the key in the front door, then footsteps and voices. They were whispering, but Dad's voice got louder as he went into the living room. I heard him opening the cupboard where he kept his whisky. Mum murmured something and Dad started yelling at her. The big night out had obviously not been a success.

I heard footsteps on the stairs and then my bedroom door opened. Mum put her head round the door and moved quietly into the middle of my room.

'Violet?' she whispered. 'Are you awake?'

I shut my eyes tight. Mum waited. Then she came padding over to my bed and bent over me. I lay still, heart thudding. After a few seconds Mum sighed and carefully felt her way back to my door.

'Night night,' she whispered on her way out.

Did that mean she knew I was faking sleep? I turned over on my tummy, feeling mean. I knew Mum longed for a proper girly daughter to confide in. But I never knew what to *say* to Mum. We didn't have a thing in common. It was almost as if *I* was the one who was adopted.

I listened to see if Mum would check out Will. She paused outside his bedroom, but then walked past to her own room. So there we were, all in separate rooms, each wide awake in the silent house.

I stared up at the ceiling. I thought about the loft up above me. Then I thought about the adjoining loft, under the same roof, where the bats were flying, their leathery little wings beating the air.

I burrowed right underneath my duvet. Phantom bats pursued me, tangling in my hair, diving down the neck of my nightdress. I huddled up tight, clasping Little Growl close to my chest for comfort. I felt so babyish, still needing to cuddle my little teddy. It was a wonder I wasn't still sucking my thumb. I dropped Little Growl overboard and lay tensely on my own, telling myself to grow up.

What was I doing, still playing these weird games with Will? Why did I always let him control me? He didn't really have any power over me. He couldn't make me do anything, not if I stood up to him. I just didn't know how to do it.

I kept to myself most of Sunday. I had a lie-in and then I had a long bath and washed my hair all over again. It's so long and thick it always takes hours to dry. The damp weight of it made my neck ache. I twisted it back in a fat plait, but I looked younger than ever then. I untied it and started experimenting, plaiting little strands of hair and tying tiny purple beads to the ends. Violet beads.

I got out my Casper Dream books and flicked through all the fairy plates. His painting of the Violet Fairy was so dark I could barely make out her hairstyle, and she was half hidden anyway behind long blades of grass. But some of the other Casper Dream fairies were very big and bright. The Sun Fairy, the Rainbow Fairy, the Rose and the Fuchsia and the Willow were all fairy princess figures with long curls flowing way past their knees. I could never decide which was my favourite. Maybe the Rose Fairy. She had little plaits amongst her golden curls, coiled intricately to form a crown around her head, studded with tiny rosebuds.

I peered hard at the painting and tried to copy her hairstyle. I didn't have any rosebuds but I had some old daisy slides from Claire's Accessories. I wove my crown of plaits, skewered them with slides, and went to look at myself in my long mirror. I sighed. I didn't look *remotely* like a Casper Dream fairy.

I pulled all the slides out, brushed my hair hard, and tied it back in one plait. I pulled on my oldest, comfiest jeans and a big baggy sweatshirt. *Will's* big baggy sweatshirt. I plucked at the soft material and then tugged it off again. I'd been wearing Will's clothes ever since I was little, his check lumberjack shirts, his navy sweaters, his stripy T-shirts. Why did I always want to wear his old cast-offs?

I put on my own blue butterfly top. It was small and

41

showed my stomach, but that didn't matter as I've always had a flat tummy. But the rest of me was still flat as a pancake too. That was the really depressing part. My chest was like a little girl's. A little *boy's*. I'd tried wearing a bra and stuffing it with tissues but it just rode up under my armpits because there was nothing to anchor it. I was a totally undeveloped freak.

Mum even took me to the doctor's to check there was nothing wrong. I had to unbutton my school blouse, nearly dying of embarrassment. The doctor just said I was a late developer, but suggested I might try exercising. I tried bending my elbows and sticking out my chest and whirling my arms around for weeks, but nothing whatsoever happened.

I tried the windmill exercise now, but my fingers kept colliding with the fairy dolls hanging from my ceiling. They bobbed about my head, doing their own aerial exercises.

Mum bought me a proper manufactured Casper Dream fairy doll one Christmas but I shut her in my cupboard. I hated all the mass-produced Casper Dream trademark fairies in gift shops and toy shops and W. H. Smith. They were horrible pouting plastic creatures with prawn-pink skins and nylon hair. They wore cheap net dresses and matching clip-on wings in stinging shades of magenta and turquoise and emerald and acid yellow.

I leafed through my books, looking at Casper Dream's subtle shades of soft purple and sea-blue and olive and primrose. I stroked the book fairies' skin, silver and sand and pearly green, and brushed their long wild curls with my fingertip. I knew Casper Dream would hate those horrible fairies flocked in their plastic cases on shelves in shopping centres. He'd hate the television cartoons too. I'd burst into tears when I saw what they'd done to Casper Dream's delicate designs and switched the set off straight away. I knew Casper Dream wouldn't be able to watch them either.

I knew him better than anyone. He knew me too. *I had a letter from him.*

Dad had bought me Casper Dream's first book, *The Smoky Fairy*, when I was six. I don't know why he chose it. He likes to say now that he had a hunch it was going to be really special, worth a fortune in the future. I think that's rubbish. Dad probably rushed into a bookshop in a hurry and picked the first little-girly book he came across.

The Smoky Fairy wasn't a big brightly coloured picture book. It's a small slim square book. I carried it around in my pocket, pretending the Smoky Fairy herself was nestled up in the silky grey lining. When all the other Casper Dream books started to get popular and Dad saw the price *The Smoky Fairy* was reaching on the Internet he made me put the book in a cellophane wrapper and store it upright on my bookshelf. Casper Dream's letter to me is carefully folded up inside it.

I wrote to him to tell him I thought *The Smoky Fairy* was the best book ever. I'd read it again and again, pointing along the lines with my finger and muttering the words until I knew them by heart. I can't properly remember everything I said in my letter. My printing was pretty wobbly and my lines wavered up and down the page. I was only six, remember. I wasn't up to giving him a detailed analysis of why I liked *The Smoky Fairy* so much.

The story was relatively simple, about a little fairy who flew in a blue-grey smoky cloud above fires or candles or cigarettes. When the flame was blown out the Smoky Fairy faded until I could barely see her glimmering on the page and I got scared she would disappear for ever, but then she made friends with a baby dragon who puffed smoke with every breath. The Smoky Fairy perched on his green scaly back and they flew away together, off the end of the page, out of the story. And I flew with them. I tried to fly literally, flapping my arms and galloping round the bedroom in my furry slippers. I must have looked such an idiot, but in my head I was the Smoky Fairy, in my own grey silky fairy dress with gossamer wings.

I have a horrible feeling I might have told Casper Dream that *I* was a fairy. I can feel my cheeks flushing even now just thinking about it. But Casper Dream was so kind. He wrote back to me, a proper letter in the same italic black handwriting as on the title page of *The Smoky Fairy*.

I unwrapped my precious copy of the book, cellophane crackling, and very carefully opened up the letter.

Dear Violet,

What a lovely name! I'm particularly fond of violets too. I shall have to invent a very special tiny violet fairy in a deep purple velvet dress. I'm so glad you like my Smoky Fairy. She's pleased too.

44

Then he'd drawn me my very own Smoky Fairy picture. The Smoky Fairy was flying, wings outstretched, her toes delicately pointed. She was waving her tiny hand at me.

Hello Violet. I wish you could come flying with me!

I wished it too. I was most impressed with my message from the Smoky Fairy and treasured Casper Dream's letter. Dad said it was nice of the chap to write back to me but he didn't make too much of it. No one had heard of Casper Dream in those days. *The Smoky Fairy* didn't attract any attention until a teacher complained that it was encouraging young children to smoke. The publishers quickly withdrew the book from the shelves. But Casper Dream's second book, a big omnibus of flower fairies, was an unexpected enormous success. It won all sorts of awards and made the best-seller lists. Lots of people started collecting Casper Dream books. Everyone wanted to find a copy of *The Smoky Fairy*, but they were few and far between. One sold for £1,000 on E-Bay. I think a signed copy sells for £5,000 now.

My copy isn't signed, but I've got my special letter. Casper Dream doesn't write letters now. I tried writing back to the address at the top of his letter but my envelope came back with 'not known at this address'. He'd obviously moved to some grand mansion with all the money he'd made. You can write to him via his publishers but you just get a fairy postcard with a printed message on the back: *'I'm very pleased you like my fairy books. With best wishes from Casper Dream.'* It's in italic handwriting but it's not hand-written. I understand. Hundreds and hundreds of people must write to Casper Dream every week.

I write to him every day. But I don't send my letters. I hide them in a big silver box at the back of my wardrobe. I squash the letters down flat but the box is nearly full now.

Dear C.D,

I can't stop writing to you. I feel as if you're my dearest friend.

It isn't as if I've made you up. You really did write me that letter. You maybe don't remember but it doesn't really matter. I know you even if you don't know me. I've pored over every shimmering page of your books so many times it's as if I know everything about you.

I wish we could meet one day.

I wish you were a real friend.

With love from
Violet
XXX

From *More Fairy Folk* by Casper Dream

Hobgoblins
Quarrelsome domestic fairies, a little dull and prosaic.

Four

I wished I could stay in my room all day like Will. Mum called me to help her peel the vegetables for lunch. She looked pale and miserable, her hair sticking up at the back because she'd obviously tossed and turned half the night.

Dad didn't get up until midday. He looked awful too, his eyes bloodshot. He smelled horribly of stale drink.

'How's my little girl?' he said thickly, putting his arms round me.

'Dad!' I said, wriggling away.

'Leave her be, Jim,' Mum said.

Dad started in on her then, a great rant about what a killjoy she was, and why did she always want to spoil everything, and what was the point of going out to a fancy dinner and dance when she'd sit there looking

49

down her nose at everyone, refusing to join in the fun?

Mum carried on peeling the potatoes, her mouth pursed up. She seemed to be taking no notice but the potato in her hand grew smaller and smaller until she whittled it right down to a nut.

Dad went on and on, getting louder. I hated him for it, but I could see how irritating it was, Mum utterly failing to respond. Her white martyred face almost invited insults. One of her eyelids was twitching. I wondered what she was thinking.

'For God's sake, Iris! Look, let me fill the kettle – I'm desperate for a cup of coffee,' said Dad, elbowing her out the way.

'I'll do it,' Mum said in a mouse-squeak.

She made Dad his coffee and handed it to him silently. Why didn't she pour it over his head? Why did she always do exactly as he said?

I thought of Will. I thought of me.

I hated thinking that I might be as meek as Mum. I started whipping up the eggs for the Yorkshire pudding, beating so hard the mixture bubbled like a Jacuzzi. I resolved I'd never let Will play games with me again.

I'd made the same resolution hundreds and hundreds of times.

I tried to take little notice of Will at lunch time. It was the one meal when he deigned to join us at the table. He ate steadily, saying nothing. Dad commandeered the conversation, eating for England in spite of his hangover – three slices of roast beef, a wedge of Yorkshire pudding, four potatoes, carrots, broccoli and peas, even

50

mopping up his gravy with a thick slice of bread. Then two servings of rhubarb crumble and custard and a cup of tea and Bourbon biscuits.

'There's nothing like a good Sunday lunch,' said Dad, belching and rubbing his stomach.

Will caught my eye and mouthed, 'Better out than in,' as Dad said it out loud. I struggled not to laugh.

Dad frowned at Will. 'Are you taking the micky?' he asked.

'As if I'd do that,' said Will. He stood up. 'Excuse me, please,' he said, and walked across the room.

'Aren't you going to offer to help your mother with the washing up?' said Dad.

Will paused. 'Help my *mother*?'

The word echoed through the air after Will had walked out.

'I don't need any help,' said Mum.

Dad stretched and belched again. 'I'm stuffed,' he said, as if someone had force-fed him the entire meal. 'I think I'll go and walk it off. Yes, let's go for a stroll, Iris?'

'I've got the dishes to do.'

'They'll keep, for God's sake. Come on, get some roses in your cheeks,' said Dad.

'Well, I'll just put the pots and pans in to soak,' said Mum, gathering up dishes.

'Oh, don't bother then, if it's so much effort,' said Dad. He patted me on the shoulder. 'Come on, Violet, you're up for a walk, aren't you, sweetheart?'

I didn't want to go for a walk at all. But I didn't want to do the dishes with Mum. I didn't want to loll in my room by myself any more. I wanted to be with Will. But he'd probably tell me to get lost if I trailed upstairs after him. And I'd only just made my firm resolution.

I grabbed my jacket and went off with Dad.

'That's my girl,' he said. 'We'll walk up to the gardens, eh?'

He used to take me there when I was little. I loved all the flowers, especially the lilies on the ornamental pond. I'd lie on my tummy in the grass, pretending Water Lily Fairies were hopping from pad to pad. I was hopefully past that stage now, but Dad was still trying to treat me like a little girl. It was a wonder he hadn't grabbed a bag of bread for me to feed the ducks. He even paused by the little playground at the entrance to the gardens.

'Fancy a swing?' he said, only half joking.

'Oh yeah, sure,' I said.

Dad picked up my hand and swung it instead. 'We've always had such fun together, you and me, Vi,' he said. His bloodshot eyes were watering. 'I wish you could stay my little girl for ever.'

'Dad.' I wriggled my hand free.

'Whoops. Sorry, darling. Don't mean to embarrass you. I forget you're a teenager.'

'Yes, well, I don't look like one, do I?' I said bitterly.

'You look lovely, sweetheart. Don't worry, you'll soon start developing.' Dad cleared his throat awkwardly. Then he smiled. 'Next time there's a big do, how about you coming along instead of your mum? She's not one for socializing. I don't suppose it's her fault, we're all different, but she does act like a bit of a killjoy. So maybe you'll be my best girl for the evening? Tell you what, there's a Masonic ladies' night next month . . . ?'

I prickled all over. I tried to keep my face under control. 'Oh, Dad. You wouldn't want me. Like, in my jeans?'

'You and your dreadful jeans! No, dozy, we'll take you shopping and buy you a really gorgeous girly dress.'

'I don't think I'm the gorgeous girly type, Dad,' I said.

I wasn't sure he was really serious. Maybe Dad wasn't sure either.

'Perhaps we'll wait a year or two,' he said, ruffling my hair. He smiled wryly. 'There, that's let you off the hook.'

I gave him a sideways glance, hurriedly trying to find a way of changing the subject. I asked him how his work was going. This was the safest bet. Dad could bore on for hours about being a policeman. His battles with chief idiots at Area Headquarters and his Neighbourhood Watch meeting with loonies obsessed with dog muck kept him burbling on all the way round the gardens and halfway back home. I switched off and thought about Will and me.

'So, what about you, Violet?' Dad said suddenly. 'How's school?'

'Oh, OK,' I said.

It wasn't OK at all. I hated school. It was so lonely. I was always such an odd-one-out. Will was too, but he liked being different. Anyway, most of the girls were desperate to hang out with him.

No one wanted to go round with me. Well, that wasn't quite true. I had Marnie and Terry. I suppose they were my friends. The only thing we had in common was our size. They were both as small as me. We were always the girls put in the front of school photos, the girls teamed up together in gym, the girls chosen to act little children or cute animals in drama. We were all three Munchkins in the school musical, and the name stuck. The other girls in our form called each of us Munchkin, as if they couldn't see any difference between the three of us.

I didn't think we looked at all alike. Marnie was really plump, with fluffy fair hair and very pink cheeks. Terry was tiny, the smallest girl in the whole school, with a brown pageboy bob. She looked about eight. She *acted* eight. They both did, forever getting the giggles and having silly arguments. They could carry on a 'Yes you did', 'Oh no I didn't' routine for ten minutes at a time.

I didn't join in the arguments. I didn't get the giggles. I didn't even talk to them much. I didn't know what to talk about because we liked such different things. Marnie and Terry got huge crushes on the latest boy pop idols, they made each other dinky little bead bracelets, they designed dream bedrooms in extreme detail, and they collected soft toys and teddies. Marnie still treasured 123 Beanie Babies and had every kind of small Manhattan toy animal. Terry collected old teddies, one-eyed limp fuzzy creatures found in corners of charity shops. Her bedroom was like a Battersea Dogs' Home for bears.

But who was I to scoff when my own bedroom was like a gothic fairy grotto? This had actually cemented my uneasy friendship with Marnie and Terry. When we were all new girls in Year Seven we'd been asked to describe our homes for an English lesson. I was stupid enough to be truthful. Mrs Mason, our English teacher, made me read my essay out loud. I had to tell the whole class about the Rose Fairy and the Crow Fairy and all the other fairy-folk. They all started snorting with laughter and flapping their arms in mock flight. I tried reading with Will-irony, one eyebrow raised, to show I knew it was ridiculous to have fairies flitting from your ceiling, but it was too late. I might be cool Will's sister but I was clearly the saddest little baby in Year Seven.

I didn't have a hope of making friends with any of the hip, stylish girls in my class. I was stuck with Marnie and Terry – and they made it clear they thought me pretty peculiar too. They were interested in the sound of my fairy-infested bedroom though, and nagged me to invite them home. I'd been to tea at Terry's house (terrified we might end up having a teddy bears' picnic with the bears in the bedroom) and I'd been to a sleep-over at Marnie's house. Marnie wore a puff-sleeved pink nightie and pink fluffy bedroom slippers. Terry wore a Care Bears nightshirt. I wore my usual big black T-shirt and black knickers. I hadn't realized we'd loll around in our night-things half the evening. I felt horribly bare. I ended up borrowing Marnie's pink quilted dressing gown, looking a total clown.

I dreaded inviting them back to my house but they were insistent. I didn't want them to go off me altogether. I didn't really like them but they were the only real friends I had. So I asked them round one

Friday. Dad was away on a 'How to Police a Major Disaster' course. The evening with Marnie and Terry turned into a domestic Major Disaster. I still go hot all over thinking about it.

I'd asked Mum of they could come round, half hoping she'd say no. But Mum seemed thrilled that I had some proper friends at last and said she'd love to have them both to tea. This started up warning signals in my head. I told her she needn't bother with a proper tea. We could have a takeaway pizza. Mum reacted as if I'd suggested we each eat a takeaway cowpat.

'I can't give guests any old takeaway rubbish,' she said.

'They're not guests, they're just two girls in my class.'

'Which two?' said Will, groaning.

I mumbled their names.

'What? You mean Tweedledum and Tweedledee?' Will said cruelly. Then he said a swear word at my stupidity and Mum sent him out of the room.

'Gladly,' said Will. 'And I'm not coming back, not while those two are twittering away.'

Will stayed resolutely in his room for Marnie and Terry's visit. They kept looking up hopefully whenever they heard his floorboards creaking. They might still frequent Bears- and Beanie-Babyland but they were boy-mad too. And especially mad about my brother Will.

It was total torture. Mum fixed one of her terrible old-fashioned high teas, the sort she had when she was a little girl, the sort *Granny* has – cold meat and crisps and salad with the radishes and tomatoes pointlessly cut into patterns, fruit salad and ice cream, then jam tarts and chocolate swiss roll and fairy cakes.

'Fairy cakes,' said Marnie, nudging Terry.

I went as red as my raspberry jam tart. They were sending me up. It was agony being sneered at by the likes of Marnie and Terry.

My fairies had been an embarrassing disappointment to them. They stared up at them, their brows wrinkled.

'They're not like *proper* fairy dolls,' said Marnie.

'I didn't realize you meant they were just little rag-dolly things,' said Terry.

'They're not dolls. They're models,' I said stiffly.

The Rose Fairy and the Crow Fairy and all their sisters dangled sadly from their strings, wings limp, heads lolling.

'Did you make them yourself, Violet?' said Marnie.

'My brother helped,' I said truthfully.

Will always cut out and sewed a tiny green satin heart for each fairy and I inserted it in each small cloth chest. But this was our special secret. I knew he'd die if I told Marnie and Terry, so I kept quiet about his contribution.

I couldn't completely protect him though. Marnie announced she was going to the bathroom. The door was open so she couldn't have mistaken it. But she walked straight past and barged her way into Will's bedroom.

'Ooh, sorry, Will – wrong room!' she squealed, and then started giggling explosively.

Terry scurried after her, going, 'Oh Marnie, trust you!'

Will slammed the door in their faces.

'Oops!' said Marnie, hand over her mouth, her shoulders still shaking.

'Why did he slam the door like that? What was he *doing*?' Terry asked.

'He wasn't doing anything, I don't *think*,' said Marnie.

They talked about Will for the next half hour, giggling all the while. I knew Will could hear everything. I knew he'd be so angry with me afterwards.

I decided to break friends with Marnie and Terry after that. I avoided them at school the next day and stalked round by myself. I knew I should try to join up with another little gang of girls but it was impossible. I couldn't just go up to someone and ask if we could be friends. I knew I could probably find Will in the library but I didn't dare seek him out. He'd made it very plain from my first day in Year Seven that we were to behave like strangers while we were at school.

So I drifted back to Marnie and Terry, because there was no one else. And now I'd given up on ever finding a congenial friend. But when I went to school the Monday after the bat weekend I got a surprise. There was a new girl in our class even though it was the middle of the term.

She was standing at the front, by Mrs Mason's desk, wearing her own clothes instead of our brown school uniform. They were amazing clothes too, a tiny black lace top, a silver and white embroidered waistcoat, a purple-velvet tiered skirt edged with crimson lace, and black pointy Goth boots with high heels. She had brightly coloured Indian bangles jingling all the way up

58

both arms and beads plaited into her hair. And what hair! Long blonde fairy princess waves all the way down to her waist.

I fell in love with her instantly.

Dear C.D,

    I keep thinking about that blonde woman who accepted your prize.

    I know you like blonde women. Nearly all the fairies and nymphs and dryads in your books are blonde, from moonbeam white to tawny yellow. I so love your picture of the Violet Fairy, but she is blonde too. I've always longed for you to create a fairy creature with long dark hair, black as midnight.

    But I do understand. Blonde hair is so beautiful.

With love from
Violet
XXX

From *Magical Creatures* by Casper Dream

The Enchantress
A sorceress; a woman versed in magical arts; a woman
whose beauty exerts irresistible influence.

Five

We all stared at this exotic new girl. She was like a love-bird amongst a flock of sparrows.

'What does she *look* like!' Marnie whispered to Terry.

'Who does she think she *is*?' Terry whispered back.

Mrs Mason was taken aback too. She narrowed her eyes as she looked at the girl, wincing slightly as if in pain.

'I know there's not much point you getting school uniform as you're only here a few weeks, but maybe you could wear something more suitable for school tomorrow?' she said.

'Sure,' said the girl, smiling.

'Only here for a few weeks? I bet she's a gypsy,' said Terry, so loudly that the girl looked over to our front row.

'Shut *up*,' I hissed, blushing. 'She's too fair to be a real Romany gypsy – and anyone else you call a traveller.'

'I'll call her whatever I want, Miss Bossyboots,' said Terry.

'Right, girls,' said Mrs Mason. 'I'd like to introduce you all to Jasmine.'

'Jasmine,' I whispered. It was the perfect name for her.

'Where are you going to sit?' said Mrs Mason, glancing round the room.

'I'll sit here,' said Jasmine pleasantly, and she walked over to my desk and sat down in the empty seat beside me.

Mrs Mason frowned. She hadn't meant that Jasmine should choose for herself, but there wasn't much she could do about it. The only other spare seat was right at the back. Jasmine sat herself down with a swish of her purple skirt and a clink of her bangles. She smelled appropriately enough of jasmine scent, sweet and strange. She smiled at me. She had the most beautiful big blue eyes, outlined with kohl so they looked even larger.

'Hi,' she said. 'What's your name?'

I swallowed, my throat nearly too dry to talk. 'Violet,' I whispered.

Jasmine laughed. 'You're kidding! Well, us flower girls had better stick together.'

'Shh, Jasmine!' said Mrs Mason. 'You're not supposed to natter in class. You're only meant to talk when you're answering a question, and then you must put up your hand.'

Jasmine said nothing, but she raised her eyebrows expressively.

'And I don't care for dumb insolence,' said Mrs Mason, going pink.

Jasmine blinked at her, looking innocently wounded, but when Mrs Mason started calling the register Jasmine muttered, 'Daft old bat.'

She had a beautiful red notebook studded with beads. She opened it and started drawing a startlingly accurate cartoon figure of Mrs Mason, adding vampire fangs and outspread bat wings.

I looked on in utter delight. She saw me staring and smiled. Mrs Mason started giving us back our English homework. Jasmine peered over my shoulder to see what mark I'd got. I was pleased that I'd got an A–. English was my best subject – well, the *only* subject I was any good at, apart from art and needlework. I'd tried especially hard analysing Mercutio's Queen Mab speech because it was about fairies.

Jasmine was reading what I'd written. I was suddenly scared she'd think me a sad swot.

'*Romeo and Juliet*?' she said.

I tried to raise my eyebrows the way she'd done. 'We had to comment on any Shakespeare passage. Boring!' I whispered, though I actually loved Shakespeare.

'Yeah, triple-boring,' she said. 'Though I don't mind the death-bed scene.' She started muttering Juliet's last speech. She did it beautifully, looking utterly stricken, as if she was truly heart-broken. Her eyes even filled with tears.

I stared at her. She blinked and then grinned.

'What?' she said.

'You know what! You did that like a real actor.'

'I *am* a real actor,' she said. 'So are my mum and dad. Miranda Cape and Jonathan Day.'

She said the names as if they were household words. I hadn't heard of either of them but I didn't like to admit this. I nodded, trying to appear impressed.

'You haven't got a clue who they are, have you?' said Jasmine.

'Well . . . Are they on television?'

'No! Well, Miranda was in *EastEnders ages* ago, and Jonathan's been several different telly cops in his time, and a few criminals too. But they're basically stage actors. They've both got big parts at the moment. Miranda's touring in a Noël Coward and Jonathan's about to open in *San Francisco*.' She saw my face. 'The musical, stupid, not the place.'

I didn't like her calling me stupid – even though she made me *feel* stupid. She talked very fast but softly, so that Mrs Mason couldn't hear. I couldn't hear properly either. It was difficult to concentrate anyway. I breathed in her strong scent and stared at her palely perfect face, her deep blue eyes, her long blonde hair. I wondered if I'd have her airy confidence if I looked like her. But maybe she could feel a little bit anxious sometimes too. I saw her nails were bitten right down to the quick. She saw me staring at her tiny chewed nails and quickly balled her hands into fists.

I didn't know what to do when the bell went for

morning break. I wanted to stay with Jasmine but I didn't want her to feel she was lumbered with me all the time. Maybe she was dying to make friends with some of the other girls. She didn't belong with me. She could be friends with anyone – Alicia, Gemma, Aisling, Lucy, all the pretty cool clever girls with designer clothes and boyfriends.

Marnie and Terry were hovering, their eyes bright with malice. I knew they were all set to have a mammoth bitch about Jasmine.

'Come on, Vi,' Marnie called.

'Over here,' said Terry, beckoning impatiently.

'Oh,' said Jasmine. She looked at me. 'Are they your friends?'

'Yes. Well, not really.' I hesitated. 'I haven't got a *real* friend,' I blurted out.

She didn't laugh at me or look at me pityingly. She gave me this big beautiful smile.

'Can't *we* be friends?' she said.

I was so thrilled I started blushing like a fool. I had to hide my red face behind my desk lid.

'*Violet!*' Marnie yelled.

'You two go on ahead,' I shouted. 'I'm going to show Jasmine round.'

I walked her around the school, showing her everything I could think of, the cloakrooms, the art room, the PE changing rooms, the science block, and each and every classroom. She tried to concentrate at first but as we went along corridors and up and down each staircase she shook her head.

'It's no use. It's a complete maze. I'll never remember it. I get all these schools mixed up.'

'So do you keep going to different schools?' I thought about my first day at Ashstead High. I'd felt sick with nerves all day, even though it was Will's school and he'd told me all about it. He did look out for me at lunch time that first day but I wouldn't go with him to the canteen because I was too scared to eat.

'Don't you mind?' I asked Jasmine.

She shrugged. 'You get used to being the New Girl. And I don't really get fussed about fitting in.' She looked down at her clothes. 'As is obvious!'

'Are you going to wear clothes like that tomorrow?'

'No, I've got an ordinary old outfit, a grey top and a green skirt. I wear that as a kind of school uniform to keep the peace.'

'You couldn't look ordinary no matter what you were wearing,' I said. I blushed again because I sounded so wet and gushing.

Jasmine giggled. She was obviously used to compliments and people getting crushes on her. A lot of the boys in our year were hovering, yelling and barging about and bashing each other, showing off to get her attention. Jasmine barely bothered to glance in their direction.

'Idiots,' she muttered.

One of them threw a KitKat at her. She caught it deftly.

'Thanks, I'm starving,' she said, opening up the wrapper. She broke a tiny mouthful off one end and then gave the rest to me.

'Hey, it's for you, not SC Violet,' the boy shouted.

Jasmine took no notice. 'Eat it,' she said to me. 'SC Violet?'

'Oh God,' I said.

I didn't want to tell her. The horrible boys in our school divided all the girls into two categories. Most of us were SCs – Sad Cows. The really pretty cool girls were SBs – Sexy Bunnies. Jasmine would be categorized as a Super-super-super SB. We all knew this was a repellent and degrading practice and all the SCs objected strongly. The SBs didn't seem to mind too much. But when I told Jasmine she screwed up her face in disgust.

'God, I can't stick boys,' she said.

'Neither can I,' I said quickly. 'Well, apart from my brother. And I'm not officially talking to him at the moment.'

'Why?'

'Oh, just because of something he did at the weekend,' I said vaguely.

'Like what?' said Jasmine.

'It's just this stupid game,' I said.

'Tell me more!'

'Nothing to tell, really,' I said. I sat down on a bench in the cloakroom and nibbled the KitKat. Jasmine sat sideways beside me, her pointy boots up on the bench. 'Have you got a brother, Jasmine? Or sisters?'

'Well. Sort of. I've got some steps and one half brother. Miranda's been married twice. Jonathan's never married but he had a son – he's grown up now. I don't like him;

he was really hateful to me whenever we had to spend a weekend together.'

'My brother can be really hateful to me too, sometimes,' I said, astonishing myself. It was as if someone else was saying my words for me, like a ventriloquist with a dummy. Then I said something even more surprising. 'My brother isn't my real brother either.'

'Is he a step or a half?'

'He's not either. My mum and dad adopted him when he was a baby.'

'So are you adopted too?' Jasmine asked, looking interested.

'No, it's just Will.' I swallowed, suddenly scared. I'd only just met Jasmine and already I was telling her everything.

'You won't tell anyone, will you?' I asked anxiously.

'Why? Is it a secret?'

'Yes! *We* didn't even know till last year, Will and me. And then our granny blurted it out last Christmas. Will was in a strop about something and she was mad at him anyway because she didn't think he'd been grateful enough for his present. It was a Manchester United shirt and Will isn't into football one bit. Anyway, she said something about bad blood will out, and what do you expect? We thought she was talking rubbish at first – she's always been a bit bonkers. But then it all came out and it was so awful.'

'For your brother?'

'Well, he acted like he couldn't care less. Like he was even glad, because he doesn't get on with our dad at all.

70

He doesn't really get on with Mum either. But Will and me, we've always been very very close. And now it's so weird, because he's still my brother, of course, but he's not *really* my brother—'

At that precise moment I looked up and there was Will walking towards us, well within earshot. I felt freeze-framed, unable to rewind. Will looked hard at me for one heart-stopping moment and then looked straight ahead. He walked right past us without saying a word.

'Who was *that*?' said Jasmine. 'He's a bit different from those other idiots. Do you like him? You've gone crimson.'

'That's Will, my brother,' I said.

Dear C.D.,

I wonder how long it takes you to create each of your wonderful books? You must sit at your drawing board all day and half the night to manage so many. Twelve books in seven years, and that's not counting the colouring books or the calendars.

Do you ever lose all sense of time?

Love from
Violet
XXX

From *The Book of Fairy Spells and Potions* by Casper Dream

A Fairy Enchantment
A charm using occult words.

Six

I didn't know if Will had heard or not. I couldn't be sure. He'd given me that one long look, but that *could* have been coincidence. Maybe he hadn't heard a word. Maybe I was just kidding myself because I couldn't bear Will to know that I'd betrayed him.

I was so enchanted with my sudden astonishing friendship with Jasmine that I didn't even want to think about Will. Jasmine and I whispered and wrote notes all through lessons and walked round arm in arm together at lunch time. Jasmine linked her arm through mine as if it was the most natural thing in the world. I'd been friends with Marnie and Terry for more than a year and we'd never linked arms once. Marnie and Terry disapproved of girls who went round cosied up together and called them stupid names.

It was so wonderful to be with Jasmine instead of Marnie and Terry.

'Come to tea with me,' she said suddenly, when the bell went for the end of school.

'I'd love to,' I said at once. 'But won't your father mind?'

'No, of course not,' said Jasmine. 'We're renting this flat near the river. It's in this big mansion block, Ellmere House. Do you know it?'

Of course I knew it. It was a wonderful dark gothic building, with many turrets and cupolas. It looked just like one of the fairy palaces in my Casper Dream books. It seemed a perfect home for someone like Jasmine. I couldn't possibly miss the chance of going to tea there, though I knew Mum would be worried sick. I didn't want to phone her. She'd fuss and want to know all about Jasmine and ask embarrassing questions. I didn't want to get bogged down in all that. I just wanted to go home with Jasmine. So I did.

I walked along beside her. I kept looking round, hoping lots of people would see me with my new friend. I saw our shadows bobbing along behind us, mine little, hers tall and slender, her long hair standing out around her head and waving in the wind. Our arms were linked again so that our shadows were Siamese twins. I pretended Jasmine's shadow was mine. I wondered what it would be like to be her. I imagined what her flat would be like, lavishly furnishing it in my imagination, giving it purple-velvet curtains and crimson sofas, scattering Persian rugs on the polished wooden floor and hanging cranberry-glass chandeliers from the ceiling.

The real flat was a disappointment, almost as beige and boring as my own house – neutral colours, corduroy-covered chairs with floral cushions, and insipid watercolour prints on the pale walls.

'Oh it's lovely,' I said politely.

'No it's not,' said Jasmine. 'None of this stuff is *ours*. It comes with the flat. It's weird, it's always the same sort of stuff no matter which flat we're in. Come into my bedroom. That's got some of *my* things in it.'

I thought it was the most wonderful bedroom in the world, although I knew Marnie and Terry would scoff. Jasmine didn't have her own television or computer, she didn't have an elaborate music player, just a little CD radio. Her strange bright beautiful clothes were hanging outside the wardrobe, transforming it. She'd covered the dressing table with glass perfume bottles and snow domes and several sets of Russian dolls, little carefully painted figures lined up in descending order right down to teeny creatures smaller than my fingernail. She'd spread an electric blue and silver Indian veil over the duvet and turned her ordinary bed into a bower. It was sewn with red jewels like rubies. When Jasmine lit the candles on her shelf the jewels glowed in the flickering light. They were scented candles, musky, sweet.

'Are they jasmine too?' I asked, sniffing appreciatively.

'They're neroli,' said Jasmine. She stretched lazily. 'It's especially relaxing. My dad used to have a girlfriend who was an aromatherapist. I really liked her. She told tarot cards as well. She said she was going to teach me how to do it. She was much nicer than Georgia, his new lady. She's just one of the dancers in the show.'

'Maybe she could teach you to dance?' I said.

'I can dance already,' said Jasmine. She put some jazzy show music on her CD player and launched into an impressive routine, strutting and sashaying, slapping her pointy boots. Her skirt whirled, showing the taut calf muscles in her slender legs, real dancer's legs.

I'd been sent to ballet classes when I was five. It was Dad's idea. He wanted a little dancer in the family. I hated the lessons. All the other little girls went to a different infants school and knew each other already. They had butterfly bobbles and diamanté hairslides and FOREVER FRIENDS necklaces and little Lycra leotards in pink and purple and blue. I didn't have any jewellery. I didn't even have a leotard at first. Mum made me change into my swimming costume for classes, even though I nearly died of embarrassment. I begged her to buy me a proper leotard but I didn't look much better when I got it. It was too big and baggy and I was always afraid it might show my bottom if I bent over.

I was in the ballet class concert that Christmas, even though I was slow to pick up the steps. Every child was in the concert, small or tall, fat or thin, talented or totally useless. I was a kitten who had lost her mitten. Dad videoed my dreadful performance. One of Will's favourite tortures was to replay me stumbling about the stage, head bowed, knees bent, wrists wringing, totally out of step with the other two kittens. It cracked him up every time.

'You're brilliant at dancing, Jasmine,' I said. 'I've always been rubbish at it.'

'I'll teach you if you like,' said Jasmine, holding out her hand.

'Absolutely not,' I said firmly.

'OK, OK,' said Jasmine, and she swapped her CD for wonderfully weird choral music.

'It's Lisa Gerrard. Isn't she great?' said Jasmine.

'It sounds very witchy.'

'It *is* witchy. I'm a white witch, didn't you know? With amazing occult powers,' said Jasmine. She flicked her fingers as if she was executing extraordinary witch spells.

'Oh yeah – and you're a vampire slayer too?' I said.

'You bet. And Supergirl. Watch me put on my special suit and fly,' she said, spreading her arms wide.

She was fooling around, of course, but she was so magical I almost believed her. I stood at her dressing table and fingered the green and blue perfume bottles and shook the snow domes and rearranged the Russian dolls, making them line up two by two in a long crocodile of best friends. I felt overpowered by perfume, shaken in a snowstorm, unscrewed into smaller and smaller pieces. I even looked different when I peered at myself in Jasmine's mirror. My eyes shone in the candle-light and when I shook my hair free of its fat school plait it tumbled past my shoulders in dark waves.

'You've got lovely hair,' said Jasmine, brushing it with a beautiful silver-backed hairbrush.

'Nowhere near as lovely as yours.'

'So we're the hairy girls as well as the flower fairy girls,' said Jasmine, and we both fell about laughing.

'I'm starving. Let's have tea,' she said.

I thought about my own tea waiting at home. I knew I should go right that minute. Or at the very least phone. But I still couldn't bear to break the spell.

'Yeah, great, let's have tea,' I said.

I thought Jasmine's dad would be in the kitchen but there was no sign of him. Jasmine rummaged in the fridge, selecting stuff.

'Where's your dad, Jasmine?' I couldn't understand why he hadn't come out to say hello. Why didn't he want to know how she'd managed on her first day at the new school? Why didn't he want to give me the once-over. My dad would have given any friend a twice- or even thrice-over.

Jasmine shrugged. 'I don't know. He's maybe at the theatre, checking stuff. There was a problem with the lighting. Or maybe he's gone out with Georgia some-place. Whatever.'

I couldn't believe she said it so casually. The tea arrangements were casual too. There was lots of luxury food in the fridge, strawberries, special cheese, asparagus, fresh prawns, Greek yoghurt, chocolate éclairs, olives, ice cream, but not the makings of a proper meal. Jasmine didn't seem bothered about proper meals. She'd had one nibble at her gift KitKat and hardly touched her school dinner. She'd just eaten a few chips and half an apple, that was all. She didn't eat properly now even though she'd said she was starving. She fixed herself a fancy little mouse-meal, one prawn, three olives, six strawberries and half an éclair. No wonder she was so slender. Her wrists were so thin her bangles clinked right down to her knuckles and she was forever hitching them back into place.

'Help yourself, Violet,' she said.

I was hungry enough to eat everything in the fridge but I matched my meal exactly to Jasmine's.

'What would you like to drink?' she said, clanking the bottles in the fridge door. She brought out a gleaming green bottle. 'White wine?'

'You're allowed to drink *wine*?'

'Sure,' said Jasmine. 'I prefer red though. We'll have that, OK? Let's take the food back into my bedroom, like a picnic.'

I took both our plates back to the bedroom, worrying about the wine. I was going to be in serious enough trouble as it was when I eventually went home. If I was also drunk I'd be grounded for ever.

'Here we go,' said Jasmine, coming into her bedroom with two big blue glass goblets filled to the brim. She gave me one and clinked hers gently against mine. 'Here's to us,' she said.

'Yes, here's to us,' I echoed. I took a deep breath and sipped my drink. Jasmine burst out laughing. It was cranberry juice.

We ate our tiny meal and drank our juice and listened to Lisa in the candlelight. Jasmine had strung Christmas tree fairy lights across the ceiling and now it was getting dark they twinkled red and green and blue and yellow. I felt as if I was in true Casper Dream fairyland.

It got darker and darker, later and later. My heart thudded when I thought of Mum. Dad would be coming home soon. If I wasn't back then he'd call out one of his police cars and start a search for me.

'I think I'll have to go home now, Jasmine.'

'No, please. Not yet. We're having fun,' said Jasmine. 'Look, I want to play you some of my other albums and show you all my drawings and stuff. Please stay.'

'I want to,' I said desperately, 'but it's really really late. I know it sounds pathetic but my mum will be so worried. You know what mums are like.'

Jasmine pulled a face, pursing her soft lips. 'Nope. Not my mum.' She said it very lightly but her voice thickened, almost as if she was going to cry.

'Your mum doesn't worry?' I said.

'Oh, she worries all right. You should see her before a first night or a telly show. You can't go near her. And she has all these little rituals. She has to wear a particular lipstick and line up her little glass animals in a certain way and swallow three sips of wine, like she's totally nuts. This isn't just when she's got a main part, she gets just as fussed if she's a fairy godmother in some silly panto or a rubbish role in a soap. And she worries about her hair and her wretched highlights and her botox injections and her tummy tuck and her boob job. She goes on and on about herself, and does she really look thin and should she go to power yoga or pilates classes?' Jasmine was spitting out the words now, her fists clenched. 'She worries all the time but she doesn't worry about me. Well, she worries that her new guy makes too much fuss of me. He's a creep, I can't stick him, he dyes his hair blond and wanders round posing all the time, you've never seen such a plonker, and yet Miranda's nuts about him. So she shoves me in boarding school out of the way, and she doesn't even listen when I phone and tell her how I hate it. Thank God Dad rescued me.'

'And are you happy now, with your dad?' I whispered.

'Yeah, of course. It's great. I love my dad. He's a truly super guy, not a bit *like* a dad. He doesn't get all heavy or tell me what to do and he acts like he's glad to have me around – but he's not here often enough. It's not his fault, he can't help it with his job. He's offered to fix me up with some sort of babysitter but I can't stand that idea. I'm fine by myself. It's not like he ever stays out all night, he always comes home, though sometimes it's not till around midnight and it can get a bit weird just sitting all by myself. I know it's daft but I get kind of ... scared.'

I gave her a big hug. Her long golden hair brushed my shoulders as if it was my hair too.

'I'd get scared. Anyone would. Look, I'd give *anything* to stay with you, Jasmine—'

'But you have to go.'

'Maybe I can stay later another time. Even sleep over,' I promised wildly. I gave her another hug and she hugged me back really hard, clinging to me.

'We really are friends, aren't we, Violet?'

'Of course we are.'

'Best friends?'

'Best friends,' I said.

The two words flickered in my head like Jasmine's fairy lights, glowing in jewel colours.

Dear C.D.,

I wonder what it's like for you, drawing and painting your magic world all day long, fairies and phantoms flying above your head? You must lose all touch with reality.

How do you cope when you come back to the real world?

Maybe your real world is magical too. I know you're very rich. I wonder what sort of house you live in now? Perhaps it's a gothic castle like the one in your pictures? You won't have pairs of disembodied hands to bring you wine and platters of fruit and draw you baths and bring you fine robes — but you'll have ordinary servants, I expect. And the blonde lady.

With love from
Violet
XXX

From *The Book of Beasts and Bogies* by Casper Dream

The Ogre
A monster who makes use of a thousand wiles to defeat and devour
the weak.

Seven

'Don't be scared now, promise,' I said, holding Jasmine's hand.

We hugged each other goodbye and then I set off. I started running as I went down the stairs, hurtling down them two or three at a time. I rushed out of the mansion block and through the landscaped gardens, slipping on the damp grass, dodging bushes and branches. *I* was the one who was scared.

I'd never been out after dark by myself. I ran nearly all the way home, hardly able to breathe when I got to my own house at last. The porch light was on. Dad was standing there at the door, arms folded.

I wanted to run right past.

There was no chance of that.

'Where the hell have you been, young lady?' he

bellowed, seizing me by the wrist and jerking me indoors. His big red fist was like a handcuff. I couldn't shake myself free. I stood blinking in the harsh light of the hall. Mum stood nervously in the background, gnawing on the back of her knuckles. She gave a little cry when she saw me. Will was sitting in the shadows halfway up the stairs. I could see the gleam in his eyes.

'Violet?' Dad shook me. 'Come on, explain yourself. You've scared us all witless. Do you have any idea what the time is?'

'Look, I think you're over-reacting. It's not *that* late. I'm fine. No need to make such a fuss,' I said, raising my eyebrows, Jasmine-style.

Will snorted, appreciating my performance.

'We thought you'd been abducted,' said Mum. 'I didn't know what to do. Will said you'd gone off with this girl from school so I phoned Marnie, I phoned Terry, but they didn't seem to know where you were.'

'He was obviously telling us a whole tissue of lies,' said Dad, glaring at Will. 'You weren't out with any girl, were you, Violet? Come on, tell the truth. I *know* you were off playing fast and loose with some boy.'

'I was with a girl, Dad. Jasmine, she's in my class.'

'The one with all the hair?' said Will. 'Is she only your age?'

'You've never mentioned a Jasmine before,' said Mum.

'You haven't got any Jasmine in your class. Stop lying, Violet. I'm trained, I can tell. Look at you, all red and shifty-eyed!'

I forced myself to look Dad straight in the face. 'Jasmine joined my class today, Dad. Come and inspect the register tomorrow if you really don't believe me. Hook me up to a lie detector, why don't you?'

'Less of the lippy attitude, madam,' said Dad. 'So what were you doing with this girl, then? Why in God's name didn't you phone home and put your mother out of her misery? You made enough fuss to be given that mobile phone so why didn't you use it?'

'The battery's flat,' I lied. 'And I asked to use Jasmine's phone but they've only just moved into the flat so they're still waiting to get a land-line installed.'

Will shook his head at my fluent lies. Mum and even Dad seemed on the brink of believing me. I gabbled on, telling them all about Jasmine's parents, making out they were still together and that I'd met both of them.

'I think I *know* Miranda Cape. Didn't she use to be in *EastEnders*? The blonde one who caused all the trouble?' said Mum. 'So what's she really like, Violet? Does she talk really common?'

'No, no, that's all an act, she's ever so posh. And so's Jonathan, Jasmine's dad. He's in *San Francisco*, that's a musical at the Rialto.'

'I saw the advert for it. I was going to get your dad to take me for our anniversary. Good lord, fancy you knowing them! And what about this Jasmine? Is she a showy little thing?'

'She's the most beautiful girl I've ever seen,' I said.

'Listen to you!' said Dad. 'Stop looking all moony, you

stupid girl. It's still no excuse staying out half the night and worrying us all to death.'

But the force had gone out of his bluster. He nagged on for ten minutes, and I meekly did the 'Yes, Dad, no, Dad, never again, Dad' routine. He subsided at last, cracking open a can of beer and settling down to watch *The Bill* on television, yelling insults at the screen whenever he felt they'd got it all wrong.

Mum asked me endless questions about Miranda and whether her hair looked naturally blonde and had she put on any weight at all and what sort of clothes was she wearing? I made it up as I went along and it seemed to keep her happy.

Will had sloped off up the stairs to his room. I sidled quietly up to my room too. I threw myself on my boring pink flowery duvet, staring up at the fairies dangling above my head. I wondered where I could find an embroidered Indian veil and a string of Christmas tree lights.

My door suddenly opened and Will walked straight in, knocking as an afterthought.

'Do you *mind*?'

'I knocked.'

'Yeah, and you gave me a lot of time to respond, didn't you?'

'So what are you up to that's so secret, eh? Writing to your precious Casper Dreamboat? Oh C.D., darling, I'm so sad and lonesome, poor little yucky me.'

'Have you been reading my letters?' I said furiously.

'How sad is it, writing hundreds of letters to a

man you've never met – and you don't even send them!'

'It's even sadder sneaking into someone's room and reading their private stuff. I think that's despicable,' I said.

'*I* think it's despicable betraying someone's birth secrets,' he snapped back, leaning against my door.

Oh god. He *had* heard. I stared at his ears, marvelling at their ability to hear a whisper at twenty paces. They were strange ears, a little pointed at the top.

'You and your Mr Spock ears,' I said weakly. I paused. 'Will, I'm sorry. I know I shouldn't have told her.'

Will shrugged. 'You can tell her what you like.'

I couldn't believe he was so cool about it. I held my hand up, high-five style. He held his hand up too and we did our old complicated slap and wave routine. Will taught it to me when I was six, when we had our own special Will-and-Violet club.

'Jasmine is my best friend now,' I said shyly. 'But she'll never be friends the way *we're* friends.'

'Yuck! Stop being so sticky and sentimental. I feel like I'm drowning in treacle,' said Will, miming scraping himself clean, but he grinned at me before walking out of my bedroom.

I couldn't be bothered to do anything boring like homework. I leafed through my Casper Dream flower fairy book instead. It was like Jasmine had flown right out of his fairyland. There were fragments of her on every page. The Bluebell Fairy had her eyes; the Gardenia Fairy had her white skin, the Water Lily Fairy her slender limbs; the Laburnum Fairy had her long fair hair. I wondered if Casper Dream made his fairies up, drawing them from his imagination, or did he have a series of elfin models tiptoeing round his studio, waving their arms and pointing their toes? Were they all one girl? Was she his girlfriend?

I looked at the dark photograph on the dust jacket. They used the same photo on every Casper Dream book, a portrait in heavy shadow, so that you could only see his eyes and his long nose and the elegant curve of his lip. It was impossible to work out how old he was. I liked to think he wasn't *too* old. If he'd created *The Smoky Fairy Book* just out of art school, when he was twenty-one or twenty-two, he could still be in his twenties now. When I was in *my* twenties the age difference would be minimal.

I didn't want to bother with silly boyfriends. I wanted to wait for the only man for me.

I asked Jasmine the next day if she'd ever had a boyfriend.

'Not exactly,' she said, giggling. 'I've let boys kiss me at parties and they've sent me Valentines and I've hung out at McDonald's with a whole bunch, you know, that sort of stuff.'

'Sure,' I said, though I'd never done any of that myself.

'But I've never been serious about any of them,' said Jasmine. 'You can't *talk* to them, not the way *we* talk.' She smiled at me.

I smiled back, my heart thudding joyfully. It was as if

we'd been best friends for years instead of twenty-four hours. Jasmine was marginally more suitably dressed today in a little grey vesty top and a tiny green skirt that showed a lot of her lovely long legs, but Mrs Mason shuddered when she saw her and called her up to her desk for a lecture on appropriate school attire.

'I should think so too,' said Marnie, sniffing. 'Honestly, you can practically see her knickers. I'd die rather than go out dressed like that. What were you *doing*, letting her hang round you all yesterday? I mean, I know she's new, but you don't have to get stuck with her. Terry thinks you *like* her, but you don't really, do you?'

'I like her ever so much, Marnie,' I said.

'But she's so full of herself,' said Marnie, pulling a silly face. 'She thinks she's *it*.'

'I think she *is* it,' I said.

'Shut up,' said Marnie. 'You're acting like you've got some kind of pervy crush on her.'

'You shut up,' I said. 'You don't understand.'

'Maybe I don't want to,' said Marnie. 'Oh well. Suit yourself. You go round with whoever you want.'

'OK. I will,' I said.

Marnie marched off to join Terry. They whispered together, glaring over at me, then tossing their heads at Jasmine.

I knew that was it as far as Marnie and Terry were concerned. They felt they'd only been friends with me under sufferance. They certainly wouldn't want to go round with me any more. But what did I care? I had Jasmine.

I knew she wasn't going to be at school long. It would be lonelier than ever after she'd gone. But I couldn't bother about that now. I had to make the most of what I'd got.

Mrs Mason finally got through lecturing Jasmine and let her go.

'Dear God,' Jasmine muttered. 'So what shall I wear tomorrow that will *really* wind her up? Oh, I know! Jonathan was once in this hilarious schoolgirl spoof set in the nineteen twenties, and he purloined some of the costumes on the last night, just for a laugh. I *think* we've still got one of the schoolgirl outfits. Oh, what bliss to come to school in a real gym tunic with black stockings and one of those black girdle thingies.'

'Jasmine Day, the Naughtiest Girl in the School,' I said.

'Come round tonight, eh? We'll work on my costume together,' said Jasmine.

'I want to – but I'm not sure I *can*,' I said, feeling awful. 'I got into trouble last night from being so late back.'

'But you weren't late. It was only about eight o'clock.'

'Jasmine, there's a drama at home if I'm ten *minutes* late.'

'Well, can I come round to your house then?'

Oh God. It had been bad enough with Marnie and Terry. I cared so much more what Jasmine thought. How would she react to my childish bedroom and all my fairies? I could always hide them away in a cupboard before she came, but without them my bedroom lost all its point. It would just be a shabby girly bedroom with faded flowery curtains, Blu-tack blotches on the walls and a sad teddy bear slouching on my windowsill.

'I'd love you to come, Jasmine, but my mum's a bit odd about me bringing friends back,' I lied.

Jasmine nodded, but she looked a little reproachful.

'I'll work on it though,' I said.

'What about your brother? Doesn't he have friends round?' she asked.

'Will's pretty anti-social at the moment. I'm sorry, my family's kind of weird.'

'I *like* weird,' said Jasmine. 'I like you, Violet.'

She really *did* seem to like me. I could say any odd thing that came into my head and she didn't back away, shaking her head, indicating I was nuts. She'd smile and act like she was really interested. I dared tell her some of my old childhood games – the tiny plasticine family I'd kept in a shoe box and carted around everywhere, the plastic mermaids I'd set swimming in a goldfish bowl, the ghost girl I was sure lived in the back of my wardrobe.

'I wish we'd known each other then. I'd have given anything to play those sort of games,' said Jasmine. 'Did you play them by yourself?'

'I played them with Will,' I said.

When he was in the right mood the little plasticine people trekked the grassy jungle of the back garden, the mermaids frolicked in the ocean with great golden whales, and the ghost girl took hold of my hand with her phantom fingers and led me into her shadowland.

'You are *so* lucky to have a brother,' said Jasmine.

But when Will was in the wrong mood he pressed my plasticine people together, mashing them into one fat pink blob, he sent my mermaids swimming out of sight right down the lavatory pan and he shut me up in the dark wardrobe with the ghost girl and locked the door.

'I don't think you understand what brothers can be like sometimes,' I said. 'Especially *my* brother.'

'Yeah, well, let me meet him,' she said. 'Come on, let's go and find him at dinner time.'

'He just slopes off by himself. I'm not allowed to talk to him, not at school,' I said.

'What do you mean, you're not allowed? The teachers don't let you?'

'No. Will won't let me,' I muttered.

Jasmine laughed. 'And you do what he says, right?'

'Will can be a bit . . . odd sometimes. If you don't do what he says then you always end up regretting it.'

She raised her eyebrows. 'We'll have to see about that,' she said.

My heart started beating fast. I knew she didn't understand. I didn't want her to get hurt.

'Don't look so worried, Vi,' said Jasmine, giving my school plait a tiny tug. 'Hey, will you plait my hair like that? Silly old Mrs Mason told me I have to have my hair tied back too. Will you be a darling and do it for me?'

'Of course,' I said. 'Have you got your silver hair-brush?'

'Not on me. Haven't you got one?'

'Yes, but it's a bit scrubby. Don't you mind?'

'Why should I? We're best friends. Your brush, my brush – your nits, my nits.'

'I haven't got nits!'

'Neither have I, silly. Come on, do my hair for me, please.'

I brushed her beautiful long golden waves. It felt so warm, so silky, so fine, compared with my thick coarse hair. My fingers were clumsy as I fiddled with each strand of plait. I was desperate to style it properly and please her.

I wasn't sure how long I'd be able to fob her off about visiting me at home. Though perhaps I didn't need to worry. Will would lock himself up in his bedroom all the time she was there. Of course he would.

Dear C.D.,

I wonder how many times I've looked at your books? And yet each time I pore over a picture I see something different.

Mum doesn't like them. She'd never look at them with me even when I was a little girl. She said the colours were too pale, too grey, too bleak. She doesn't like the trees with their gnarled faces and long twisted roots. She thinks the warty old witches and the pop-eyed ogres and the fire-breathing dragons and slithering serpents are too frightening for a child's book.

'Don't blame me if they give you nightmares,' she said.

They did give me nightmares, but I didn't care.

One time I went barging into my bedroom and Mum was sitting on my bed, your book open on her lap. She looked startled, jumped up, and started dusting, her back to me. But I'd already seen the tears running down her cheeks.

I couldn't work out why.

With love from
Violet
XXX

From *Fairies of the House and Hearthside* by Casper Dream

The Hearth Fairy
A timid sprite who tries to bring goodwill to the household.

Eight

We were going to spend all of Saturday together, Jasmine and I. I loved saying those three words. Jasmine-and-I. It was as if we were permanently hyphenated together, Siamese soul-sisters.

Jasmine told me to come over to her flat as early as possible on Saturday morning.

'Can you be there by ten? And stay for lunch and supper too, please please please. We'll do whatever you like, Violet. We don't have to stay in. You can show me all the good shops in town or we can even have a day up in London, wherever. I'll pay, I've got loads of cash. It's guilt money – Miranda's started sending me wads of cash and Jonathan's been pretty generous recently too. Still, he's doing well with *San Francisco*, they're extending the run for a whole season – isn't that

101

fabulous! It means I can stay for three months, maybe even more.'

'Maybe it'll be like that Agatha Christie play that ran for fifty years?'

'Yeah, right, so we'll be best friends all our teenage years and go to college together and get a flat and compare notes on our boyfriends—'

'But we won't ever live with any of them, and we absolutely definitely won't get married.'

'Absolutely definitely. Marriage sucks,' said Jasmine. 'You're so lucky, your mum and dad staying together.'

'Yes, but they don't get on. It only works because Mum gives in to Dad all the time. Jasmine . . . can't we stay friends after you move away? We could text each other and e-mail and maybe see each other some weekends?' My voice went a bit wobbly. I didn't want to sound too keen, too needy. But Jasmine smiled radiantly, her eyes bright blue.

'Will you *really* keep in touch? All the girls I've gone round with promise they'll stay friends. They write back to me once or twice but then they just fade out of the picture.'

'I won't fade. I shall stay shining in the corner.'

'There's this hymn my granny used to sing, about a little candle burning bright, and it ends, "You in your small corner, and I in mine." I loved my gran so much. She looked after me when I was a baby, and then I stayed with her for a bit when Jonathan and Miranda first split up. She sat me on her lap and cuddled me and called me her little bunny. She was so lovely lovely lovely. I'd give anything to have her back. She died a year ago and I wept for a whole week.' There were tears in her eyes now, and one spilled down her cheek. I gently wiped it away with the cuff of my cardigan.

'Thanks, Violet. Is your gran still alive?'

'Yes. But I wish she was dead,' I said.

Jasmine blinked at me. More tears spilled but she wiped them away herself. '*What?*'

'I know it's wicked but I can't help it. Don't be shocked.'

'Why do you hate her?'

'She was the one who told Will he was adopted. I *told* you.'

'I wonder why they adopted him?'

'I don't know. I mean, they can obviously have their own children because they had me.'

'Maybe they thought they couldn't. You came along like a little surprise later on.'

'Maybe.' I gave a little shiver.

Jasmine laughed. 'You're thinking about them doing it, aren't you?'

'Jasmine! Yes, I *was*. How do you know everything about me? I mean, I've been friends with Marnie and Terry for ages but they don't have a clue.'

'Yeah, well. They're not your best friend. I am. And it's all fixed for us to spend the whole of Saturday together, yes?'

'Yes,' I said, though I thought I'd have great trouble sorting it out. I usually did a big shop with Mum on

Saturday morning. She liked to finish off with a slice of cake and a cup of tea in Marks and Spencer's café and she'd smile at me eagerly and say, 'Isn't this fun?' It wasn't my idea of fun but I acted like I was really enjoying myself because I didn't want to hurt her feelings.

I had to act on Saturday afternoons too if Dad was around. He liked me to clean the car with him. I'd been doing this ever since I was a little kid, when I really did find it fun messing around with a hosepipe and a lot of foam.

Will had once been part of the Saturday stint, though he was frequently in trouble. He'd juggle with oranges or balance loo-rolls on his head or run amok with the shopping trolley, and whine for more cake and spill his drink down himself. Mum would tell him off constantly and try to bribe him to behave. Dad just got furious with him. Once Will deliberately turned the hosepipe on him and Dad lost his temper altogether and walloped him.

It was a relief all round when Will got to eleven or twelve and flatly refused to join in Saturday jaunts, holing up in his room with his homework. *I* was still expected to play happy families even now I was thirteen.

I couldn't psych myself up to saying anything about Jasmine's invitation until breakfast. Then I announced it, just like that.

'I'm going over to Jasmine's,' I said, and I took a quick sip of tea. I was so tense that I choked, and Mum had to pat me on the back.

'You've got ever so pally with her in a very short space of time,' she said. 'I don't really know why she wants to see so much of you, Violet. I mean, we're just ordinary folk and they're celebrities.'

'Why *shouldn't* this Jasmine want our Violet for her friend?' said Dad. 'She's obviously got good taste. You go and have a good time, Violet. I'll come and pick you up at lunch time.'

'I'm staying there for lunch, Dad.'

'Well, tea time then. I'd like to meet her.'

I couldn't stand the thought of Dad barging into their flat and acting all heavy-handed with Jasmine. He'd given Marnie and Terry a ludicrous warning about never taking E tablets at dances, but they are so hopelessly uncool Terry thought he meant *vitamin* E tablets. I had always felt I was equally sad and out of it, but now Jasmine had picked me out to be her best friend it was as if a little of her dazzle had sparked off something in me.

'Oh *Dad*,' I said, and I raised my eyebrows. 'It's OK, Jasmine says *her* dad will give me a lift back sometime this evening.'

'Jonathan Day's giving you a lift! And I expect he's got a really posh car too,' said Mum.

'Well, make sure he hasn't been drinking. I know what some of these actors are like. We had one of the *San Francisco* cast let himself down the other night – absolutely paralytic, he was. One of our lads caught him taking a leak in someone's front garden. That's not very nice, is it?'

'It keeps foxes away,' said Mum. 'Don't stare at me l
ike that. It stops them digging up your garden.'

'What does?' said Dad.

'Men's urine,' said Mum, pronouncing it delicately
and then blushing.

'Well, you're a mine of information, Iris,' said Dad. He
caught my eye and grinned, wanting to make a joke of
it, us against Mum. I grinned back guiltily because I
needed Dad on my side.

I thought Will was still asleep. He often slept late at
weekends, not coming to forage for his breakfast until
midday. But when I went upstairs to get my jacket he
came out onto the landing in his old towelling dressing
gown, hair tousled, feet bare.

'Where are you off to, so bright and early?' he said,
nodding at my jacket.

'I'm going to Jasmine's,' I said proudly.

'Ooh, how jolly jolly jolly,' he said in a silly girly gush.

I looked at his pale face, at the dark circles under his
eyes. He was obviously mocking me, but I wondered if
he wished he was going out to see a friend? Did he really
want to be such a loner?

I suddenly felt so sorry for him I wanted to give him
a big hug.

Will wrinkled his nose and backed away from me.
'Get away from me, Violet. You stink!'

I was wearing jasmine scent. I'd bought my own little
bottle.

'I don't stink!' I said, hurt.

He was the one who stank, smelling of unwashed boy

and rumpled bedclothes. He yawned and stretched, scratching his tousled hair.

'I was thinking. We haven't had a hike through Brompton Woods for ages. Fancy a tramp?'

I stared at Will. Once, long ago, he had taken me on a magical day out to Brompton Woods. We'd caught the bus to Brompton village and then walked for miles under a vast canopy of old oaks. It rained on and off but the branches above our heads were so thick with leaves they acted as umbrellas.

I had the Dragonfly Fairy in my pocket, her turquoise gossamer wings carefully folded. I reached into my pocket every now and then to stroke her. Will led us along tiny winding paths in the woods. I followed obediently because I was little enough then to think he always knew where he was going. He took us to a secret green pool in the heart of the woods, with real dragon-flies skimming the emerald water. Will felt for the Dragonfly Fairy in my pocket. He made her shake her wings out and then he ran with her round and round the pond.

I know he must have held onto her all the time, but somehow I remember her swooping independently, soaring along on her iridescent wings, her green legs running through thin air.

I'd begged and begged Will to take me back to that pond in Brompton Woods. Sometimes he said he was too busy. Sometimes he said I was mad wanting to go all that way just to see some old stagnant pond. The last time I'd asked him he'd looked at me vaguely and said,

'Brompton Woods? Have we ever been there? I haven't got a clue where they are.'

He was waiting now, his eyes gleaming, almost as green as the pond.

'Let's go tomorrow,' I said.

'I can't tomorrow. I've got plans,' said Will. 'Today.'

'But *I've* got plans, Will. You know I'm going to Jasmine's.'

'Go there tomorrow,' said Will.

I thought it out in my head. I could phone Jasmine, make up a headache, a tummy upset, some family crisis. She'd understand. I saw Will and me walking through the woods, finding the green pond. I was too old for Dragonfly Fairy games but I could still take her in my pocket like a lucky mascot.

Will had a little smile on his face, reading my thoughts. He knew me so well.

But I knew him too. I knew why he was doing this to me. I also knew that as soon as I'd cancelled everything with Jasmine he'd start wavering. He'd come up with some excuse why we couldn't go to Brompton Woods after all. He might not even bother to make it plausible.

I was sick of Will's power games.

Maybe I'd sooner see Jasmine than Will.

I would *much* sooner see Jasmine.

'I'm seeing Jasmine today, Will,' I said.

I walked past him, along the landing. He didn't call after me. I didn't look back.

I wanted to go to Jasmine's straight away. It was only

nine but I didn't think she'd mind. She'd begged me to come as early as I could.

'At least let me give you a lift there,' said Dad.

There was no way I could get out of this one. I didn't want to be alone with Dad, especially as he was still going on about Mum, ridiculing her.

'She's ludicrously impressed by this new friend of yours and her fancy actor parents,' said Dad. He exaggerated the word – act-*or* – in fruity tones, as if he felt this was the way actors themselves would say it. 'What sort of car does this Jonathan whatsit drive, then?'

'*I* don't know, Dad.'

'I thought you said he gave you a lift home the other evening?'

'Yeah, he did, but you know I don't know one kind of car from another.'

'Well, was it big and flash?'

'It was just . . . ordinary,' I said vaguely.

'Honestly, Violet. You've got the powers of observation of a gnat.'

'Yeah, well, I've not been professionally trained like *some* people,' I said.

'So what are *you* going to do when you grow up, darling? Still into this sewing lark, eh? Sister Susie's sewing shirts for soldiers. Well, I suppose you can always sew your dad a few shirts.'

'I don't want to sew shirts, Dad. I want to design stuff. You know. Like my fairies.'

Dad sighed, and then reached out and patted my hand. 'I think you're away with the fairies half the time,

Violet. You're such a dreamy girl. Still, it's good for you that you've got this Jasmine. Your mother and I have been worried about you not having any friends. I know you went around with those little dumpy girls but you didn't seem that happy in their company.'

'I'm not friends with them any more. I just want to be friends with Jasmine.'

'Well, I should be a bit cautious. Strikes me it's best to have lots of friends. Then if one or t'other lets you down you've always got half a dozen other mates. Like all my lads at work or the Masons or the guys at the golf club.' Dad smiled smugly as he showed off his own popularity. 'Still, this friendship with Jasmine is a start. You need to branch out more. You don't want to moulder at home and just tag after Will.'

I glanced at Dad. He was staring straight ahead, watching the road.

'Don't you want Will and me to be friends, Dad?' I said softly.

He didn't answer, humming along to some old pop tune on Radio 2. Maybe he hadn't heard me. Maybe he was *pretending* he hadn't heard me.

'Of course I want you two to get on together,' Dad suddenly blurted out. 'It's just I don't like the way Will bosses you about and encourages you to join in all his silly games.'

'What games?' I said, a pulse beating in my forehead. Ghostly bats flew straight in my face.

'Silly looks, sighs, dumb insolence, all that nonsense,' said Dad.

I breathed out slowly. 'He's going through a stage,' I said.

'He's always been in some bloody stage,' said Dad, through clenched teeth.

'Why don't you like him, Dad?' I said.

'What? What do you mean? Of course I like him. He's my son.'

'Is it because he's adopted?'

'For God's sake, Violet, don't start all that. And don't you dare bring this up with your mother. She scarcely slept for weeks after *my* bloody mother let the cat out of the bag.'

'But *why* didn't you tell Will before? It must have been so awful for him finding out like that.'

'He was the one *acting* awful as far as I remember, refusing to say thank you for his present. Wasn't that how it all started, Will being bloody-minded and selfish, as always? I know your gran winds people up. Dear God, she winds me up enough. But Will didn't have to be downright rude to her. What was it he said? Smelly old bag? How dare he!'

'I know he was rude. But I just don't understand. How could you and Mum keep it a secret all these years?'

'It wasn't really a secret, as such. We were going to tell him as soon as he was old enough to understand. But by that time – well, your mother thought of him as *her* son and it would have been so painful for her. She wasn't well, not for a long time, after—' Dad swerved suddenly to avoid a bike. 'Good God, where did he come from?

111

Look, Violet, I don't want to talk about it any more, especially not when I'm driving. I don't want to kill us both.'

'But Dad—'

'The subject's closed!' Dad said sharply.

We didn't say another word until we got to Jasmine's flat.

Dear C.D.,

I wonder what you were like when you were a little boy? I know you must have loved drawing right from when you could first hold a pencil. Did your parents encourage you? I wonder about your father — maybe he wouldn't have liked seeing you hunched up over a drawing pad, creating your own private fairy world? Did he nag you to go out and play football like the other little boys?

He must be so proud of you now though.

With love from
Violet
XXX

From *The Book of Fairy Poetry* by Casper Dream

The Elf King
The king of elfs, and the little fairy queen
Gamboll'd on heaths, and danc'd on every green.

Nine

Jasmine came to the door in a velvet patchwork dressing gown and threw her arms round me in delighted surprise.

'How lovely you're here so early. We're still having breakfast. Come and have some.'

I had a second breakfast with Jasmine and Jonathan. He was so different from my dad, from anyone else's dad. He was this cool thin fantastic guy with longish tousled fair hair, in jeans and a grey T-shirt. Will's kind of clothes, but less rumpled and saggy, probably an expensive designer version. There was nothing remotely saggy about Jonathan. His T-shirt was tight fitting, with very short sleeves, showing off his carefully toned muscles and flat stomach.

'Hi, Violet. Wonderful name!' he said, as if *I* was

wonderful too. 'I've heard so much about you already. You and Jasmine are obviously great friends.'

'Yes, we are,' I said happily.

'She's a lovely girl, my daughter, isn't she?' said Jonathan.

'Dad!' said Jasmine, rolling her eyes. 'Shut up!'

Jonathan didn't seem to mind at all. He just pulled a funny face, miming zipping his mouth – though he talked non stop throughout breakfast. He told some slightly silly joke and I laughed obediently, but Jasmine put her head on one side and said, 'Come again, Dad? That's meant to be *funny*?' Jonathan pretended to be upset, hanging his head, and Jasmine laughed and ruffled his fair hair, calling him a poor old love.

She talked a lot too, telling him all about school, going on about Marnie and Terry, and she swore, a real four-letter word, but Jonathan didn't turn a hair. I imagined telling my dad to shut up, ticking him off for making stupid jokes, ruffling his hair, swearing straight in his face. It was impossible. I simply wouldn't dare.

I didn't dare say much to Jonathan either because I was so shy. He was very patient, asking me stuff about my family. I answered monosyllabically and he tactfully changed the subject. He talked about me instead, asking me what I liked to do most.

'I sew,' I said. I'd sewn Jasmine a present but I felt too shy to give it to her straight away, especially in front of her father.

'What sort of sewing? My girlfriend Georgia does tapestry.'

'I just sew . . . small stuff. And I look at books a lot.'

'Fantastic! I hope you turn my Jas into a bookworm, Violet. She's a shocker. I'd read all of Shakespeare and most of Dickens when I was her age but she can barely stagger through Harry Potter. What's *your* favourite book, Violet? You look like a girl who'd like a little gothic passion. Have you read *Jane Eyre*?'

I *had* read *Jane Eyre*, and loved it too, but I didn't want to say so in case it looked as if I was ganging up on Jasmine. She didn't seem to mind particularly.

'You're just trying to impress Violet, Dad. I bet *you* haven't read *Jane Eyre*. You've just read the stupid telly script.'

'It was an excellent script and I was a superbly sexy Rochester,' said Jonathan, striking a dark and glowering pose.

'You, *sexy*, Dad?' said Jasmine laughing. 'Not with your hair dyed black and those ridiculous tight breeches.'

'I was sexy with nobs on, saucebox,' said Jonathan. 'The girls playing Jane Eyre and Blanche Ingram thought so. I had my work cut out keeping them both happy.'

'Oh God, we're boasting now,' said Jasmine, pouring me another cup of coffee from the cafetière.

We had Nescafé at home, with Gold Blend for visitors, and breakfast was cornflakes and toast. Jasmine and Jonathan had croissants and pink grapefruit juice and a bowl of cherries. I ate them too, savouring each mouthful, wishing I could be part of their family for ever.

Then Jonathan started reading the *Stage* newspaper and Jasmine took my hand and led me off to her room. When we were on our own I took a deep breath and then produced her present from my jacket pocket.

'A present!' said Jasmine, clasping the little pink tissue parcel and untying the green silk ribbon.

'Don't get too excited. It's nothing much. You'll probably think it's stupid,' I said anxiously. I wanted to snatch the parcel back. How could I have been so childish? Jasmine seemed light years older than me. She wouldn't want my silly little gift. She'd raise her eyebrows and laugh at me.

'Look, it's daft. Please, give it back to me,' I said, reaching for the parcel.

'No! It's mine. Hands off,' said Jasmine, opening it up. Her fingernails were the same pearly-pink shade as the tissue paper. She edged it wide open and then looked, silently.

I'd made her a fairy. I'd stayed up late sewing her the last three nights. I'd refined my usual pattern, making the basic shape extra slender, separating the fingers and pointing the toes. It made stuffing her very tricky. I had to use a pin to get the kapok right down to the end. The first time she looked a little lumpy so I scraped her out and started again. The face caused me trouble too. I didn't want to stylize the features. No little black French knot eyes and simple backstitch smiley mouth for this doll. I painted a face very carefully and then filled in the tiny eyes and mouth with satin stitch. I plaited silky fair embroidery thread, sewed them onto the soft little scalp, dozens and dozens of them, and then gently teased them out into fluffy curls.

The costume was a problem. I wanted it white and gold, with a hint of pink, but I didn't have any material remotely like that in my scrap box. I used white silk in the end, shading it with rouge and sprinkling a little gold glitter here and there. I made the wings out of white feathers with two pale pink and one primrose on the underside, barely showing.

She was the best fairy I'd ever made but when I looked at her in her nest of tissue she was just an embarrassing little toy, lumpy and home-made.

'A Jasmine Fairy,' Jasmine whispered, cupping her in her hands.

It was as if she'd breathed life into her. The Jasmine Fairy quivered, ready to fly.

'Where did you *find* her?' said Jasmine.

'I made her,' I said.

'You made her specially for me? Oh Violet, you're the most perfect friend in all the world.'

'No I'm not,' I mumbled, all choked up.

'She has *wings*,' said Jasmine, waving her around.

'There's some very fine elastic in the tissue. We can attach her to your lightshade. She'll look like she's flying there.'

I helped her get the Jasmine Fairy organized so she drifted above our heads, arms outstretched, dainty feet pointed. I blew on her and she twirled round and round, her wings lifting, her curls waving gently round her shoulders.

119

'She is so wonderful. Are you going to make one for you too?'

'I've got lots at home.'

'Have you made a Violet Fairy? Then they can be friends and fly together. So what can I give *you* for a present?'

'I don't want anything.'

'You've got to have something. What have I got?' Jasmine seized her red and purple outfit from where it was lying crumpled on the floor. 'How about these? You said you liked them.'

'They're yours! And I couldn't wear that sort of thing, they'd look all wrong on me,' I said.

'No they wouldn't, but I suppose they would be a bit big for you,' said Jasmine. 'Choose a perfume bottle then. Or a snow globe? Go on, choose several, I'd love you to have them. Or what about my Indian bangles? You like them, don't you?' She started pulling them all off her arms.

'No, don't, Jasmine. I couldn't possibly take them. Well, maybe just one? Not to keep, just to borrow for a bit.'

'Have them all, Violet. No, I know, half! You know little kids have those FOREVER FRIENDS lockets and break them in half? Well, we'll each wear half the bangles, OK? You can have all the purple ones to match your name.'

'Well, if you really don't mind? But it *is* just a borrow.'

'No, it's a gift,' said Jasmine. She threaded six brilliant bangles on my left wrist and the other six on her own. I shook my arm experimentally. They jangled a little tune. Jasmine shook her own arm.

'We sound like a percussion band,' I said. 'Oh Jasmine, I *love* them.'

I loved them especially because it made us look like sisters.

We stayed in Jasmine's room all morning, lounging on her bed and listening to her music. She told me stories of all the other schools she'd been to while travelling round with Jonathan. She was especially vitriolic about her boarding school.

'Marnock Heights was an absolute *prison* of a place, and so old fashioned. Talk about Jolly Hockey Sticks! The gym mistress was a really scary lady with this moustache and she beat me with her horrible hockey stick.'

'She *beat* you?'

'Well, threatened to. I hated it there, it was so awful, and the food was total rubbish too so I stopped eating and this mad matron started giving me lectures about the dangers of anorexia, for God's sake. If they'd given me a halfway decent meal I'd have fallen on it ravenously, but who wants to eat slimy shepherd's pie or rice piddly pudding? I kept phoning Miranda, begging her to let me come back home, but all she did was whine about having to pay for the wretched phone calls. So I phoned Jonathan, even though I was mad at him at the time for walking out on Mum and me. He was at the school in a matter of *hours*, all set to rescue me. The headteacher protested but Jonathan wouldn't let the old bat wear him down. He didn't argue, he just switched on the charm. And I packed my bags in double-quick time and then we were *out* of there.'

Jasmine jumped up, acting it out. 'It was so sweet of Jonathan too, because he'd just fallen madly in love with this fashion model – you know, Bija, the one with blue hair and the diamond in her teeth? He knew a schoolgirl daughter would disrupt their little love nest but he said he didn't care. He said *I* was far more important. Isn't that fantastic?'

I murmured appreciatively, finding it totally bizarre that a *dad* could be having an affair with someone incredibly famous and beautiful like Bija. Jasmine told me more and more extraordinary tales about all these parties she'd been to with Jonathan. She said she'd sung a duet with Robbie and borrowed Kylie's lipstick and read bedtime stories to Brooklyn and Romeo. I drank it all in, sure she was making most of it up now but not caring. I just wanted to hang onto her hand and be whizzed around this extraordinary new world.

She couldn't really be on singing/borrowing/story-telling terms with all these celebrities. But when Jonathan took us out for lunch *we* were treated like celebrities. We didn't go anywhere ultra posh – there *isn't* anywhere ultra posh in Kingtown – but I was thrilled to sit with Jasmine and Jonathan in the window at Pizza Express. *Three* different women in the restaurant come over to ask for Jonathan's autograph and told him how much they liked the show. Then a teenage boy came over and murmured something in Jasmine's ear, blushing. I stared, mouth open. Jasmine stayed totally cool. She wrote her name on a crumpled paper napkin with a flourish.

'He wanted your autograph?' I said.

'Yeah, only because he thinks I'm a dancer in the show. Bless!' said Jasmine complacently.

'But you're not!'

'Not *yet*. Give me a couple of years!'

'Over my dead body,' said Jonathan. 'You're going to be a good sensible girl and stay on at school and go to university and get yourself properly educated. I don't want you staggering across stages or camping it up in front of the camera. I want you to have a serious, fulfilling career. Let's drink to that.' He poured a little of his half bottle of white wine into Jasmine's glass and mine and raised his own glass.

I felt pleasantly sophisticated toasting Jasmine's future. It wasn't the first time I'd tried alcohol. I'd shared a can or two of lager secretly with Will and I'd drunk champagne at a wedding, but this was my first legitimate small splash of wine. I sipped it happily. One of Dad's colleagues went past outside on his way to the station to start his late turn. He did a double take when he saw me. Then he spotted Jonathan and gawped all over again. I smiled back demurely through the glass. It was as if Jonathan and Jasmine and I were on a celebrity chat show on television with everyone watching us.

Jonathan treated us both so specially too. It wasn't just the wine, it was the way he talked to us like adults, looking us in the eye and listening to everything we said. He asked our opinions and seemed to take them seriously. It was as if we really mattered to him. I stopped feeling so shy. Maybe the few sips of wine helped a little.

Jasmine told Jonathan I liked Shakespeare. She shuddered as if she were saying slugs and snails. Jonathan told us really funny stories about playing Bottom in *A Midsummer Night's Dream* at an open-air theatre. It rained solidly night after night. Bottom's donkey head started to grow green slime all over its fur and the ears started to droop pathetically. I asked what costumes the fairies wore.

'Hey, Jonathan, Violet's made me a little fairy doll,' said Jasmine.

'I love fairies,' said Jonathan.

I looked at him warily, scared he might be sending me up, but he seemed completely genuine.

'Remember I took you to that special fairy shop, Jas? How old would you have been? About five? Maybe six? We bought you a bright-pink frock with wings and you wouldn't stop twirling round. You thought you were the bee's knees.'

'You bought me a silver wand to go with it and when I went back to Miranda's she called me her little Sugar Plum Fairy. Then that horrible Mikey, one of the steps, kept calling me the Sugar Bum Fairy, and I got so cross I poked him in the eye with my wand,' said Jasmine, spluttering with laughter.

'You watch out for my daughter, Violet,' said Jonathan. 'She looks such a sweet little sugar lump but she can be a very bad girl indeed. Fairy Princess turns straight into Wicked Witch. I worked on some new Grimm adaptations a couple of Christmases ago. It was a special kids' show but the Grimm was *very* grim and frightened them into fits. The stage set was pretty scary too, very very dark with lots of gnarled old trees with faces, like those Casper Dream fairy books.'

'Casper Dream!'

'Yeah, fantastic artist. Do you like his books, Violet?'

'I *love* them. They mean all the world to me.' I stopped. They were both staring at me. 'I – I mean, they *did*, ages ago, when I was just a little kid.'

'I nearly got to play him once,' said Jonathan.

Now *I* was the one who stared. 'Does Casper Dream look like you then, Jonathan?' I asked hoarsely.

'No one knows. He's a bit of a recluse. He just stays indoors chained to his desk, illuminating his fancy manuscripts like a medieval monk,' said Jonathan, miming it all.

'Have you met him?'

'No one has. This TV company wanted to do an hour's special programme on his life and work and approached his publishers. Their publicity people were really keen but apparently he wouldn't hear of it. He never gives interviews. So then they rejigged the original idea, interspersing critical appraisal of his work with dramatized scenes—'

'Of you being the medieval monk figure?' said Jasmine, smiling at him.

'Yeah, yeah, so what's so funny? There were going to be animations of his work, maybe a few girls dressed as fairies. Very tastefully – this was a serious arts show.'

'Even so, I don't think he'd like the idea of animations and people dressed up,' I said.

'That's right. He still wouldn't hear of it. I tried to find out where he lives to see if I could go and plead with him personally. I'm a big fan of his books, I've got lots of them. Well, not his first little book – *nobody's* got that. Anyway, no one knows where he lives. Even his publishers don't seem too sure. It's as if he's as elusive as his own fairies. He won't phone or e-mail anyone, ever.'

He wrote to *me*, I thought, with a secret shiver of pleasure. He put his address on the letter. I knew where he used to live. If only I'd tried harder to see his house I might even have spotted him. I'd begged Dad to drive me there, but he said it was a crazy idea, and he had a hundred and one more pressing things to do than stalk some artist clear across three counties.

'I've got *The Smoky Fairy Book*,' I said.

'Has it been reissued?' said Jonathan eagerly. 'Oh boy, I've got to get hold of it.'

'No, I've got the original one.'

'The first edition? But the print run was so small – and then it was withdrawn because of all the cigarette fuss. How did you get hold of it? Are you *sure* it's a proper first?'

'I think so. It was given to me as a present when I was seven.'

'I hope you didn't scribble all over it!'

'No, of course I didn't,' I said, a little hurt. 'I didn't ever scribble in my books.'

'Jasmine did. Well, you lucky, lucky girl! I'll have to have a peep at it some time.'

'Let's go round to your place now, Violet,' said Jasmine. 'You can show Dad this old book and me all your other fairies.'

Jonathan looked at his watch. 'I can't, sweetheart. I've got the matinée at three.'

'Your boring old matinées! Oh well, *we* can still go round to your place, Violet,' said Jasmine.

I thought of Dad with his feet up on the sofa, shoes kicked off so that the whole living room smelled of his socks. Will once held his nose as he walked past and Dad got furious and lectured him for half an hour on rude and childish behaviour. Mum would go horribly shy and practically bob curtsies – but then she'd run Jasmine down behind her back. And Will . . .? Will disliked all my friends. Look at the way he'd behaved with Marnie and Terry. He was in a bad mood with me anyway because I'd chosen to go over to Jasmine's rather than go out with him. He'd be working on a way of getting his own back. I didn't want to risk him taking it out on Jasmine.

'It's a bit of a madhouse at my place on Saturdays. It's my mum, she does all her housework and turns everything upside down.' It wasn't really a lie. Mum did her housework *every* day and took it very seriously. 'I think we'd better stay well clear or we might get roped in to help.'

'OK, you've talked me out of it,' said Jasmine. 'But some other time soon, please, Violet?'

127

'Yes, of course,' I said, wondering how I was going to fob her off for ever.

'Violet would far rather come and watch me in my matinée,' said Jonathan, holding his arms up in an actorly attitude.

'Oh yeah, sure,' said Jasmine.

'I *would* like to see you act,' I said politely to Jonathan.

'Then come to the theatre with me, darlings. We'll wangle you the best seats.'

'She's just being tactful, Pa,' said Jasmine.

'No, really, I want to,' I said. 'I love the theatre.'

'I knew you would!' said Jonathan.

I hoped he'd never find out that my only experience of the theatre so far was the pantomime at Christmas. We went on a terrible police family outing. There was a very camp guy playing Widow Twanky, who kept pretending to swoon at the sight of so many policemen in the audience. Dad started getting edgy about it and called out, heckling him. Mum and Will and I wanted to crawl under our seats and hide.

It was strange walking up to the theatre and seeing Jonathan's name up over the entrance and his big black-and-white face smiling down at us. I started to walk into the foyer but he steered me round to the stage door down the side of the theatre. It was much shabbier inside than I'd expected, and there wasn't very much to marvel at, just endless pale-green corridors and flights of cord-carpeted steps.

However, Jonathan's dressing-room lived up to expectations. He had one of those star-style mirrors with

128

lights all round, with a photo of Jasmine tucked into the frame. There were several different glamorous girls grinning at him from heart-shaped photo frames, boxes of chocolates and baskets of fruit, and a big casket spilling stage make-up.

Jasmine helped herself to a plum and started experimenting with purple eyeshadow. Then she got started on me, outlining my eyes with black pencil and painting my lips crimson.

'What do I look like!' I protested, but I was really thrilled. I didn't look like my vague shadowy self any more. I was more defined, as if Jasmine had outlined me all over.

Jonathan sat at his mirror in his T-shirt, expertly applying panstick. He didn't seem the slightest bit nervous. I knew if I had to stand up on stage and act in front of an audience I'd have been shaking with terror.

Jasmine and I left him to change into his stage clothes and went to our seats.

'The *best* seats,' said Jasmine.

I expected two seats in the stalls but Jasmine threaded her way through more complicated corridors, had a quick conversation with someone, and then led me up the stairs and opened a little door.

'Oh wow! We're in a box!' I said.

It was incredible sitting there staring right down at the stage, cut off from the rest of the audience in our special red-plush world. I leaned forward, holding onto the gilt rail, and saw several people staring up at me, as if *I* was famous. Then the music started, the lights went up, and

Jonathan came strutting on stage. He sang, he danced, and when he triumphantly finished his opening number he gave Jasmine and me a jaunty wave. We waved back, as if we were about to step right into the show.

Dear C.D.,

I wonder how many letters I've written to you? It must be hundreds and hundreds. I started off on torn-out pieces of notepad, pencilling in big letters, my lines sloping crazily up and down the page. Then I progressed to proper teddy-bear notepaper, and I crayonned on all the bears, giving them little wings to turn them into teddy fairies. Then I went through a Kitty phase, and there were the rainbow letters, and the time I was so into stickers each letter was heavily embossed.

I fancied you probably had some overseas hideaway castle so I started using thin blue airmail letters. I've sent you postcards too, any I can find with fairies, though none are as beautiful as yours. I've drawn you my own fairies too. And I always draw me at the end.

Love from
Violet
XXX

From *The Weird Book of Witches, Boggarts and Bogies* by
Casper Dream

The Black Witch
A woman who practises malicious magic or sorcery,
believed to have dealings with the devil.

Ten

'You sat in a box!' said Mum at breakfast the next day.

'It's not that big a deal,' said Dad. 'It's just a chair in a little balcony, for God's sake.' He yawned and stirred his cornflakes. 'I'm sick of this mushy stuff. Why can't we have a decent cooked breakfast, a bit of egg and bacon and sausage?'

'You know why. You're the one with high cholesterol,' said Mum. 'Fried breakfasts aren't good for you.'

'Just one day a week, that's all. My mother used to make fabulous fry-ups every morning. No one could beat her fried bread or her fried potatoes!' Dad smacked his lips wistfully. 'And she's still fit as a fiddle, even though she's . . .' He paused, squinting at the calendar on the wall. 'Oh God! It's not the eighteenth today, is it?'

'Yes,' said Mum, sounding a little defiant.

'It's the old bat's birthday, isn't it? And we haven't got her anything.' Dad looked at Mum reproachfully.

'But I didn't think, seeing as we're not really on speaking terms any more . . .' Mum didn't finish, but she glanced at Will.

He was standing by the breadbin, working his way through slice after slice of bread and strawberry jam. He didn't pause in his spreading and munching routine, but he chewed more rapidly, as if he had difficulty swallowing.

'Yeah yeah, I haven't forgotten,' said Dad impatiently. 'I haven't got Alzheimer's. Come to think of it, that's maybe how she came out with all that spiel. She's quite likely losing the plot, going a bit demented.'

'That old witch knew what she was doing all right,' said Mum, with uncharacteristic venom.

'Don't start calling my mother names,' said Dad.

'You were the one who called her an old bat,' said Mum, chin up.

'There are bats next door,' I said quickly.

They both looked at me, surprised. Will was looking at me too.

'What did you say?' Dad asked.

'Bats. There are lots of them. I think they're roosting in the loft.'

'Oh God,' said Mum, dabbing at her hair. It was still tumbled round the shoulders of her blue dressing gown, so that from the back she looked as young as me. But her face was pale and lined, especially between her eyebrows and at the corners of her mouth. She'd tensed so often the lines stayed, even when she rubbed her fore-head hard with her fingertips. I wondered if she'd look any younger married to someone like Jonathan.

'I can't stick bats,' Mum fussed. 'I *knew* something like this would happen. Why on earth doesn't that niece *sell* the house? I think we should call in the council.'

'Bats are a protected species,' said Will. 'They've got squatter's rights.'

'Don't be silly. They're vermin,' said Mum.

'He's right, actually,' said Dad, though he sounded reluctant to admit this. 'The bats have to stay. There's nothing we can do.'

'But they'll get into our house if we're not careful,' said Mum, combing her hair with her fingers and secur-ing it in a knot on the top of her head. 'How many bats did you see, Violet? Were they flying all round the garden?'

'Mmm,' I said vaguely.

'Don't you go out in the back garden with your hair loose then,' said Mum. 'They get tangled in long hair.'

'That's a complete myth,' said Will. 'There are hardly any recorded instances. Bats are interesting, I've been reading up about them – they're not blind either, they can distinguish light, especially sunrise and sunset, though their eyes aren't very developed—'

'OK, OK, Mr Smarty-Pants-Swallowed-the-Encyclo-paedia, we all know that. They find their way round using radar,' said Dad.

'No, they use sonar, actually,' said Will.

'I'm not the slightest bit interested in what they use,'

said Dad. 'How did we get started on this bat business anyway? Come on, we'd better get cracking, all of us.'

'Why?' said Mum, retying her hair even tighter.

'We'll have to make a trip to Mum's. Get some flowers and a big box of chocolates on the way.'

'You're not serious?' said Mum.

'Look, she's an old lady. She's maybe not going to *have* many more birthdays.'

'She's not *that* old. Make up your mind. First she's fit as a fiddle, then she's half daft, now you've got her on her last legs—'

'OK, OK. Look, all I'm asking is we go over there as a family. It's a nice drive, for God's sake. We won't stay. We'll just have a quick coffee and then we'll go and find a decent pub and have a Sunday roast.'

'*We've* got a Sunday roast. I bought a leg of lamb.'

'So, we'll have a *Monday* roast. Go on, you nip up and use the bathroom first,' said Dad, and when Mum got up he patted her on her bottom, presumably helping her on her way.

I wanted Mum to slap his hand away, but she gave him a little smirky smile that made me feel sick.

I hated her being content with so little. She didn't seem to care that Dad had no respect for her whatsoever. If he put on his police boots and commanded her to lie down she'd probably let him trample all over her.

I thought of Will and me. I felt even sicker. Didn't I do exactly what he said? Apart from yesterday. And now he was trying to make me pay for choosing to see Jasmine. He'd been ignoring me ever since.

To hell with Will, I thought. But when I looked over at him my chest went tight. I saw the hunch of his shoulders now that Mum had given in.

'What about Will, Dad?' I said.

'What about him?' said Dad.

'You can't expect Will to come and wish Gran a happy birthday, not after all those things she said.'

'She'll likely have forgotten all about it by now,' said Dad.

'Will hasn't forgotten,' I said. 'Think what it will be like for him.'

Dad sighed in exasperation. 'I couldn't give a stuff what Will thinks,' he said, acting as if he couldn't even see the boy chewing jam sandwiches beside him.

'The feeling's mutual,' said Will, with his mouth full.

'Less of the lip, lad. Go on, get cracking, put a decent outfit on, not those awful scruffy jeans – and don't wear that necklace either.'

Will didn't budge. He spread himself another jam sandwich.

'For God's sake,' said Dad, slamming his hand down on the kitchen table, making the plates jiggle. 'Stop stuffing that big mouth of yours and get ready to visit your gran.'

Will waited until he'd cut his sandwich. He took a mouthful. Then he said very calmly, 'I'm not coming.'

'Of course you're bloody coming,' Dad thundered, standing up.

'Of course I'm doing no such thing,' said Will.

'You'll do as I say, lad, or—'

'Or?' Will repeated.

Dad stood in front of Will. They were exactly the same height now. Dad was much the heavier, built like a barn door, but Will was wiry and surprisingly strong. Dad took a small step forward. Will stepped forward too, so they were comically close, noses almost touching. Will went right on chewing.

'Can't you eat with your mouth shut? You've got the manners of an animal,' said Dad. He edged around Will, and started to clear the table. 'OK then, *don't* come. See if we care,' he said. 'Come on, Violet, get these dishes washed up and then go into the bathroom after your mother.'

'I'm not coming either, Dad,' I said.

Dad stopped. He was still holding a cup and saucer. He slammed them down so hard that the handle snapped straight off the cup. Dad hung onto it, hardly noticing.

'This is all your fault,' he said, glaring at Will. 'What sort of example are you to your sister?'

'She's not my sister – as her grandmother pointed out so charmlessly,' said Will.

'I *am* your sister,' I said. 'And I don't want to see Gran ever again.'

'Violet.' Dad came over to me, shaking his head. 'Stop this nonsense. Now go and get ready, sweetheart.' He reached out as if he was going to give me the same proprietorial pat on the bottom he'd given Mum. I swerved away from him.

'Don't, Dad! I mean it. I'm not coming,' I said.

Colour flooded Dad's face. I saw the pulse beating at his temple. He raised his arm again and this time I thought he was going to slap me. I clenched my fists and stood my ground. Dad let his hand fall to his side without making contact.

'Stay at home, then,' he said. 'I'm not going to waste my breath arguing with either of you. You make me sick, the pair of you.' He turned on his heel and started to march out of the kitchen, but he was wearing his old scuffed slippers. He tripped and one slipper twisted sideways. He didn't stop to sort it out, he walked on anyway, step shuffle, step shuffle, until he was out the door.

Will and I looked at each other and then cracked up laughing, hands over our mouths to muffle it or he'd be back and *really* slapping us about. Will made another strawberry jam sandwich, taking great care this time, even cutting off the crusts. He arranged it on a plate in dainty triangles and then offered it to me with a flourish. I ate it up in eight quick bites.

'So it looks like we have a day to ourselves,' said Will.

'I thought you said you had plans for today,' I said.

'I could cancel them,' said Will, grinning.

'Maybe we could go to Brompton Woods,' I said. 'Oh Will, please let's.'

'Maybe. Later on. We can see what we feel like.'

'OK. Only . . . don't feel like playing any games, will you?'

'Games can be fun.'

'Blind Man's Buff isn't my idea of fun.'

'I'll invent a new game for your delight.'

139

'For *your* delight, you mean.'

'Exactly. Or what would be the point?' said Will, his eyes glittering.

I looked at him warily, wondering what little game he was hatching. 'We are friends now, aren't we?' I said.

'Of course we are.' Will dug his finger in the strawberry jampot and smeared my wrist and his own with scarlet jam. 'We'll still be blood siblings,' he said, and then he licked my wrist clean and I licked his.

Mum made a fuss when she came downstairs in her green woollen dress, a purple scarf pinned into place with an amber brooch. Her face was very pale above her colourful outfit.

'What's all this about you not coming? Of *course* you're coming – both of you.'

'No, we're not,' said Will. 'And you don't want to either. You're just going because Dad bullied you into it. Gran's never been that nice to you either, has she?'

Mum flushed, looking uncomfortable. 'Don't, Will, please. All right, you don't have to come. I do understand. But Violet, you must go. You'll upset your dad so if you don't.'

'That's just too bad,' I said, folding my arms. I kept them folded, hugging myself for courage when Dad came back downstairs. His face was still bright pink, his neck nearly purple where his tight collar was digging into him. He always dressed in a formal shirt and tie and suit to see Gran because she said she couldn't bear seeing grown men in sloppy T-shirts.

'Last chance, Violet,' Dad said. 'We're leaving in five

minutes. You've still got time to get washed and get your togs on if you jump to it.'

'I'm not jumping, Dad,' I said.

'Right,' said Dad. 'I'm not going to lower myself and plead. Though what if this is the last birthday your grandmother ever has? It's surely not too much to ask, one little family visit on a special day, after all I do for you? I even act like your personal chauffeur, driving you round to see your fancy friends.'

I stood silently, hanging onto my elbows, trying not to react.

'You stone-faced little cow,' Dad said suddenly. 'What sort of a daughter are you? Well, stew in your own juice then.'

He stormed out of the house. Mum gazed at us anxiously, fumbling in her purse and putting a ten-pound note down on the table.

'There's not much in the fridge apart from the lamb and stuff. Get yourselves something nice down at the corner shop. And don't do anything silly, either of you. Do you hear me?'

I nodded, suddenly near tears.

'Don't worry, I'll look after her,' said Will.

Dad yelled from out in the driveway for Mum to get a bloody move on.

'Hark at him, bellowing like a bull. What will the neighbours think?' said Mum. 'I've half a mind to stay home too.'

But she scuttled out to join him. We heard the car doors slam and then the roar of the engine as they drove off.

It was very quiet in the kitchen. Will tore a kitchen towel off the roll and gently dabbed at my wet eyes.

'I'm crying because of Mum, not Dad,' I sniffed. 'You're lucky, Will. I wish he wasn't my real dad. I hate him. If only I had a dad like Jonathan.' But I shut my mouth quickly. I didn't want to spoil things by talking about Jasmine and annoying Will.

'Cheer up, little sister,' said Will.

'Oh Will!' I sobbed.

'Hey, you won't need a shower at this rate. Race you for the bathroom, eh?'

Will got there long before me, but he was only two minutes using the bathroom. I took much longer, washing my hair in the bath. I heard music coming from Will's room, beautiful strange piano playing. He usually played really loud thumping rock music, partly to annoy Dad, but I knew he had a collection of classical CDs that he listened to secretly, using headphones.

When I was dressed I pattered shyly along to his room, my hair tied up in a towel. Will had propped the door open so I could hear the music properly.

'It's lovely. What is it?'

'Debussy. It's called "The Dance of Puck". It's the nearest I can get to fairy music for you.'

I hovered at Will's door. 'Can I come in?'

'Sure.'

It was ages since I'd been in Will's bedroom. Muffy's cage was still there, taking up half the room. He'd tied black ribbon and white silk lilies to the bars and made a model of a chinchilla out of papier-mâché, painting it white and putting it on a pedestal so it looked like a marble memorial statue.

'Oh Will. You *must* get another.'

'No, no more pets. I'm not keeping anything caged any more. I'm getting into bats though. I've made a bat box and hung it out the back of our house. I want them to roost in *our* loft.'

'You are joking, aren't you?' I *thought* he was, but I saw he had several library books on bats. He had piles of books all over his room, mostly non-fiction, but he had a lot of fantasy and horror paperbacks and there were all his old childhood favourites still on the windowsill, the Narnia books and *The Wind in the Willows* and *The Jungle Book*. There were reminders of the little boy Will all over his room. He'd kept his quartz collection, and the same little troop of pipe-cleaner mountaineers were trekking up this rocky terrain. I looked all round and eventually spotted Big Growl hibernating under a pile of crumpled clothes.

The pictures and postcards Blu-tacked to his walls were more sophisticated, mostly photos of tortured Gothic singers, boys in black with black hair, girls in white with long blonde hair. There was a set of Hieronymus Bosch creatures with rabbit heads and flowering genitals coupling in imaginative new ways, then a painful series of souls being tortured in hell. There were also five photos of Muffy crouching in corners, her snout in the air, her eyes bright with love. The only other photo was one of a baby, a peaky little creature with a shock of thick black hair and big violet eyes.

'You've got *my* photo on your wall!' I said.

'Well. You were quite sweet then. You've gone off rapidly since,' said Will.

'I looked so weird as a baby. It's odd, we are a bit alike. Look at the hair.'

'I always used to wonder why there weren't any baby photos of me,' said Will. 'I asked them once. Dad said it was because I was such an ugly little tyke that the camera broke. Mum got a bit flustered and spun me this long story about a photo album going missing. I was more inclined to believe the old man.'

'What – that you were ugly?' I said.

'Well, I am,' said Will, lying back on his bed, his arms behind his head.

'Oh, come *on*! You're milking the poor-little-me situation a bit too much now. You know perfectly well everyone things you're drop-dead gorgeous,' I said.

'What do you think, Violet? No, OK, we're related, more or less. What about little friend Goldilocks? You two obviously have long discussions about me.'

'No, we don't. Well. Just the once.'

'And what did she say about me?'

'*I* don't know.'

I did know. Jasmine had said he seemed the only interesting boy in the whole school. But that was private, between Jasmine and me. She'd die if I told Will, I was sure.

'I think we'll maybe play a game of Truth or Dare,' said Will.

'Oh God,' I said.

'Don't look so panic-stricken. It'll be fun.'

'For you. No, Will, let's go out, please. We don't have to go all the way to Brompton Woods. We could go anywhere. We could just have a little wander in the park, or go round the shops. We've got Mum's tenner, look. We could have lunch in McDonald's. Or I'll cook us lunch. *I* could do the roast, I'm sure I could, though I'll have to get started right this minute.'

'You go and make us a coffee while I ponder,' said Will.

'OK, great, coffee coming up,' I said, shooting straight down to the kitchen. I made us both black coffees and I snaffled two truffles from Mum's secret supply in the tablecloth drawer. She always hid her birthday boxes of chocolates because Will and Dad would help themselves indiscriminately if she left them out on the sideboard.

Will came downstairs when I called, ate his truffle and then mine too. I decided not to object. I made burbling small-talk, switching on the television and flicking from channel to channel, suggesting we play an old game where we turned the sound down and acted out madly surreal voiceovers. Will was exceptionally good at this. I hoped he might want to show off but he shook his head. He drained his coffee, and leaned back in the upright chair, rocking it precariously on two legs.

'OK, we've had our light refreshments. Now it's Jolly Japes time. Right, little Shrinking Violet, we'll play Truth or Dare.'

'Will, stop it. It's a ridiculous game. And anyway, you don't ever tell the truth, and I'm useless at dares.'

145

'Which should add considerably to the fun! Come on, indulge me. Then we'll go out. We'll buy a picnic at Waitrose and get the bus to Brompton Woods, OK?'

'Promise?'

'Well, it depends. Indulge me now, and then we'll see.'

'I don't want to play, Will. I hate games.'

'But we've never played Truth or Dare. Don't worry, it won't be the ordinary kids' game. It'll be my special variation.'

'Which makes it much more scary.'

Will bowed as if I was complimenting him, grinning at me. He had very good white teeth but there always seemed rather a lot of them, giving him a disconcerting wolfish look. When I was little and Will played around threatening to eat me up I took it very seriously.

He rocked on his chair, almost but never quite overbalancing.

'First Truth or Dare challenge, Violet. If you could have a love affair with anyone, who would you choose?'

I felt as if I was overbalancing myself. This was a very different kind of game. Will never seemed the slightest bit interested in my feelings and we'd never discussed love in our lives. I'd often *wanted* to, and long ago when we shared secrets I'd try to start Will off on the subject, but he'd always groan and make vomit noises and tell me not to be so boring.

'You're hesitating, Violet. Come along, we'd better introduce a time limit,' said Will, going to the kitchen and getting Mum's timer. 'OK,' he said, returning. He adjusted the clock mechanism. 'You have precisely sixty seconds in which to answer. Failure to come up with a truthful response or an acceptance of a dare means you will have to pay a dire penalty. Mmm, I shall enjoy making one up.' He sat back on his chair, chanting, 'Tick tick tick.'

My thoughts ticked over in time. I remembered going to nursery school and some scruffy little boy with a skin-head haircut taking a shine to me. He said he loved me. I lied and said I loved him too, to be polite, though I didn't like his stubbly head, or his nose-picking habits. 'That's good,' he said, exploring his nose thoroughly. 'So we'll get married, right?'

'I can't,' I said, too shocked to stay polite. 'I'm going to marry my brother Will.'

When I got old enough to know I couldn't marry Will I decided I didn't ever want anyone else. Will didn't seem particularly interested in going out with any girls when he got into his teens so I had wistful fantasies about us sharing a flat together.

Now *I* was in my teens I could see this probably wouldn't work. I wasn't sure whether I wanted to go out with anyone, let alone have a love affair. I thought of all the boys at school. Jasmine was right, they were all rubbish.

I thought of Jasmine. I loved her, but not in that way.

'Tick tick tick, ten seconds left. Penalty looming,' Will said.

'Shut up, I can't think.' I shut my eyes tight to concentrate. Coloured lights danced behind my eyelids. When I was little Will told me these were fairy lights. I spent hours with my hands over my eyes, trying to see them more clearly.

'Fifty-seven, fifty-eight—'

Fairies!

'I know! Casper Dream,' I said triumphantly, as the timer went off.

Will frowned. 'He's not a real person.'

'Of course he is.'

'You don't know him. You don't even know what he looks like. That photo on his books is all blurry.'

'I don't need to know him. I still choose him.'

'OK, OK,' said Will, sighing.

'So who would *you* choose, Will? Come on, it's my turn to play Truth or Dare. Who would you choose for a love affair?'

I set the timer and looked at Will. His eyes were very green, staring back at me without blinking. His face was impassive, utterly Zen-cool. I couldn't wait to hear what he'd say. I sat forward eagerly, holding my breath. Then the phone started ringing, making us both jump.

'Leave it,' said Will.

'But what if it's Mum checking up on us? She'll come back if we don't answer.'

Will frowned and picked up the phone. He listened for a second – then held out the phone. 'Jasmine,' he said.

The timer went off, the sound filling the whole kitchen.

Dear C.D,

Did you have lots of friends when you were at school? Maybe some of the tough kids teased you because you were quiet and sensitive and so very talented at art?

I expect you had one very special friend?

I wonder if it was another boy?

Did you really care about him?

Did you trust him?

Did you stay friends? I really really want to know.

Love from
Violet
XXX

From *Shadowlands* by Casper Dream

The Wraith
A spectral apparition of a person about to die.

Eleven

'I'm sorry, Jasmine, but I can't really talk right now,' I said quickly.

'Yes, you can,' said Will. 'What does she want, your friend Jasmine?'

Jasmine giggled at the other end of the phone. 'I can hear your brother! Look, I want some help with my homework. I can't do *any* of it. Especially the maths.'

'Oh Jasmine, I'm useless at maths too,' I said.

'I'm not,' said Will. 'Tell her to come round. I'll help her.'

I stared at him. He didn't seem to be joking.

'What did he say?' said Jasmine. 'Did he say I can come round?'

'Well—'

'It's sixteen Heathland Road, right? I'll get Jonathan to run me over. OK?'

I looked at Will. 'Do you *want* her to come over?' I mouthed.

'Is this another Truth or Dare?' said Will.

'What?' said Jasmine. 'What are you two on about? Anyway, see you in ten minutes? Your mum won't mind, will she, Violet? I know you said she gets a bit funny about stuff.'

'My mum's gone out. And my dad,' I said. I swallowed. 'They're out all day, actually.'

'Oh great. So we can have a party, you, me and your brother,' said Jasmine.

There was a little pause.

'I'm *joking*, Violet,' said Jasmine. 'OK, see you soon!'

I put the phone down. The plastic was slippery. I wiped my hands on my jeans, looking at Will. He looked back at me steadily.

'Why did you ask her round?' I said.

'Why shouldn't she come round? She's your friend,' said Will.

'But you always hate my friends.'

'I hate little Munchkin friends. Jasmine looks like she'll be more fun.'

'Will, don't play games with her.'

'As if I would,' said Will, his eyes glittering.

'Don't spoil everything, Will. It's been so lovely this morning, the way it used to be. I wish she wasn't coming. I wanted it to be just you and me.'

'And now it'll be just you and me and Jasmine,' said Will. 'It'll be fine. Don't look so fussed. I'll be nice to your new friend.'

'Really?'

'Really and truly,' said Will.

I reached out and squeezed his hand gratefully. Will's hand was strangely damp too. He wasn't usually a sweaty anxious person. Maybe he was just picking up on my emotions. I felt so worried about Jasmine coming over. I scurried up to my bedroom, reaching up and setting all my fairies swinging. Maybe she'd think me an idiot, stringing a lot of limp rag dolls from the ceiling. No, she loved her own Jasmine Fairy, she said so. But was she simply being kind to me? Or even having a little laugh behind my back, like Marnie and Terry?

I stroked my collection of Casper Dream books. She wouldn't laugh at them. Jonathan had been so impressed that I had *The Smoky Fairy*. I could show Jasmine all my favourite colour plates. Or would she be bored, looking at books? I didn't really know. She was my best friend but I didn't really know her properly at all.

I ran out of my bedroom, slamming the door shut. I hurried downstairs, into the living room. I smoothed the sofa, shoving all the scattered Sunday papers into a heap, finding Dad's awful slippers and stuffing them out of sight.

'It's your best friend who's coming, not the Tidy Police,' said Will, following me. He flopped onto the newly tidied sofa. 'God, look at you. You're worse than Mum.'

'Look, you could help! It was you who invited her,' I said, whisking things around. 'And get off that sofa – I shall have to plump up the cushions all over again. Jasmine will be sitting there.'

'Oh my, golly gosh, I didn't *realize*,' said Will, leaping up. 'Shall I restuff each cushion while we're at it? Cover them with cloth-of-gold? Nothing is too good for the Jasmine bottom.'

'Shut up,' I said, swatting him with one of the newspapers. Then I caught sight of myself in the mirror above the mantelpiece. I was still wearing my towel turban and old jeans and an ancient check shirt of Will's. I gave a little shriek and ran back upstairs.

'Oh my, are we off to tart ourselves up for the royal visitor?' said Will.

But when I dashed downstairs again in my butterfly T-shirt and best jeans, my damp hair brushed out, bangles jingling on my arm, I saw that Will had changed out of his old tracky bottoms and torn T-shirt into his black jeans and a brand-new white T-shirt straight out of the packet. He wore his silver necklace round his neck – and he'd actually brushed his hair.

I was touched that he was trying so hard for me. We sat in our finery on the newly plumped sofa. And sat and sat and sat. I kept peering at the clock, leaping up every time I heard a car nearby, but Jasmine failed to appear.

Will eventually burst out laughing the tenth time I leaped up. 'For God's sake, Violet!'

'She said ten minutes! It's nearly three quarters of an hour. Where do you think she's got to?'

I was so anxious, desperate for her to get here. Yet I also couldn't help hoping she wouldn't come at all. Part of me wanted the phone to ring and Jasmine to tell me she couldn't make it after all. I didn't know why. I didn't think I needed to worry too much about Will. He seemed to be trying really hard to be on his best behaviour. He could be so beguiling when he wanted. I knew Jasmine didn't seem to like boys, but she'd actually said she quite liked the look of Will, hadn't she? It would be so perfect if we could all get on together, Will and Jasmine and me.

So why was my heart beating hard under the butterfly wings on my T-shirt? Why was I staring at the phone, willing Jasmine to ring with some excuse?

I thought of all my fairies, the Dragonfly, the Rose, the Willow, the Crow Fairy, and in my head I set them spinning, scattering fairy dust.

'*Ring!*' I wished – and the phone started ringing.

'She's not coming after all,' I said, running to the phone.

'Yes she is,' said Will. 'You wait.'

'Hi, Violet,' said Jasmine on the phone, her voice wavering because she was speaking on a mobile. 'Sorry, slight delay. I decided to get a bit of food seeing as we're having this party and I had to wait for the shops to open. I'll be with you in ten minutes – and I *mean* ten minutes this time. OK?'

'Yes. Sure. Lovely. See you soon,' I said, and put the phone down.

I looked at Will.

'I'm always right,' he said smugly.

'How?'

'I'm magic.'

'Yeah.'

'The changeling child. The dark fairy goblin who disrupts family life. The child who saddens the mother and infuriates the father and terrorizes his little sister.'

'Oh yes, help, help, you're frightening me,' I said, trying to turn it into a joke. 'I wish you wouldn't go on about being a changeling, Will, it's sick.' But seeing him lounging on the sofa, even in his good clothes with his hair brushed, there was still something unearthly about his white skin and black hair and glittery green eyes, something savage about his big gleaming teeth, something strange about his bare feet with their long toes and pointed nails . . .

'*Cut* your nails, why don't you?' I said irritably.

'Right now? So that the princess arrives while I'm hacking at them with your sewing scissors?'

'Do you really use my scissors to cut your toenails? That's disgusting! And I wondered why they got blunt so quickly.'

We were still bickering noisily when the doorbell rang at last. Jasmine stood smiling on the doorstep, weighed down with huge carrier bags.

'Hi! Here's the picnic!' she said. 'Shall I take the bags into your kitchen?'

She looked incredible, wearing a tight black low-cut top edged with lace, a pale pink and primrose flouncy silk skirt, and her black high-heeled boots. She was wearing one armful of bangles and a new home-made necklace, my Jasmine Fairy hanging from a long black velvet ribbon.

'Doesn't she look lovely?' said Jasmine, giving the fairy a little flick with her fingers. 'You're so clever, Violet.'

I was pleased she liked the Jasmine Fairy so much, but disconcerted to see her worn as a necklace. It made her more of an object, a pretty little ornament. I didn't like to see her tied up, hanging on the ribbon, even though Jasmine had attached her very neatly. She'd tied a matching black velvet ribbon round the end of one tiny plait, but the rest of her hair hung loose and shining to her waist. I reached out my hand as I followed her, longing to slide my fingers down those golden curls.

'Is it through here?' said Jasmine. 'Isn't your house neat and tidy! Jonathan and I are such slobs, we never get the place straightened up. Oh wow, look at your kitchen, it's gleaming! And it all looks brand new. Have you just had it fitted?'

'My dad did most of it.'

'*My* dad can't even bang in a nail without knocking a wall down – *and* ending up in Casualty,' said Jasmine. She started unpacking her bags, producing the most amazing luxury food – lobster, king prawns, chicken breasts, flans, salads, baguettes and brioches, chocolate cake, cream cakes, a pineapple, melon, peaches . . .

'Jasmine! There's heaps and heaps!'

'Well, it can be tea as well as lunch. And I thought maybe your brother's got a big appetite. Will he

157

really help me with my homework, do you think?'

'Maybe,' said Will, standing in the kitchen doorway.

He wasn't staring at the feast spilling out over the entire kitchen unit. He was staring at Jasmine. She was staring straight back at him.

The kitchen was very quiet apart from the *tick tick* of the timer clock. The fridge suddenly switched itself on and made us all jump.

'Is this for all of us?' said Will, reaching for a peach.

'Do you dare to eat it?' said Jasmine.

Will looked impressed because she was quoting from his beloved T. S. Eliot. She probably didn't know the poem at all, quoting at random from some play Jonathan had been in.

'Oh, I dare all right,' said Will, sinking his teeth into the peach. A little juice ran down his hand. He licked his fingers.

'Will, stop eating. It's only half past eleven,' I snapped.

'I'm hungry,' said Will.

'You can't be. You had all that bread and jam at breakfast.'

'I *love* bread and jam,' said Jasmine. 'My granny used to make her own raspberry jam. It was so good.'

'Home-made jam doesn't count. Or nutritious brown bread. The true bread and jam aficionado demands limp white sliced bread and synthetic scarlet jam.'

'Or how about chocolate spread?' said Jasmine. 'Or, I know, that thick sweet milk you get in tins. We had it once when we went camping, Jonathan and me.'

158

'Condensed milk! *Excellent* choice. I can't imagine you shivering in a sleeping bag, rain dripping down on your canvas roof.'

'That's Boy Scout camping. Though I bet you weren't ever a Boy Scout.'

'I'm certain you weren't a Brownie.'

'No, I wasn't that sort of girl.'

They seemed to have forgotten I was in the kitchen too.

'I went to Brownies once,' I said. 'I thought it might have something to do with fairies. How sad is that!'

Jasmine and Will didn't react at all, not even to laugh at me.

'We could have a coffee now,' I said, putting the kettle on. I scurried round the kitchen, getting out the best rose-patterned cups and saucers, hunting for a jug for the milk, rifling through the cutlery drawer for the special silver sugar spoon . . .

'Oh for God's sake, Violet, stop faffing about,' said Will, spooning instant coffee into three big mugs. 'Let's have the cake now anyway.'

'Chocolate cake,' said Jasmine, ripping open the packet.

Will cut the cake with the breadknife, hacking it into clumsy wedges. 'Here,' he said, handing the biggest slice to Jasmine.

'Great,' she said, taking a large bite.

I'd only ever seen her nibble at food before – one bite, sometimes just one little lick – but now she chewed her way through the great big slice, seemingly relishing it.

Will gave me a big slice too but I was feeling too anxious to eat.

'So what about your homework, Jasmine?' I said, trying to make things normal. 'Is it just the maths, or all of it? I could maybe help you with the history or the French.'

'Give it here,' said Will. 'Seeing as Violet's bottom of the class in practically everything.'

'I'm not! Only maths. And I'm nearly top in art.'

'What about you, Will? You're top in just about everything, aren't you?'

Will shrugged. 'Have you been going on about me, Vi?'

'Everyone goes on about you at school. I've heard heaps of stuff about you already,' said Jasmine.

'Yeah, well, I expect it's all rubbish,' said Will. 'Let's see this maths then.'

Jasmine fished her school stuff from her big suede shoulder bag. Will peered at the set questions.

'Right. Piece of cake. Now, I can explain it all properly, show you how to do it, then you can work all the sums out for yourself—'

'Or you can just tell me the answers,' said Jasmine.

'OK,' said Will.

She started writing them down as he dictated. I hesitated, and then ran to get my maths homework book too.

'Violet, I rather think Miss Rushbrook will smell a rat if you get your sums all right,' said Will. 'You do your own work.'

160

'Oh poor Violet, don't be so mean to her!' said Jasmine. 'Come on, Vi, you copy off me.'

So I copied too while Will worked everything out for us. He was so patient, so pleasant. The rare times I'd persuaded him to help me before, he'd always been so ratty and patronizing. He was great with history too, giving Jasmine an entire essay plan with all the points she needed to make. He was fun with French homework, pretending to be French himself, putting a tea cosy sideways on his head like a beret and grabbing a baguette in each hand, conducting with them while he made Jasmine and me recite our way through our vocabulary lists. Jasmine was pretty useless at French but she was brilliant at improvising in a passable accent. Half the things she said were just made-up words but they sounded impressive.

We carried on talking in silly French accents when we started eating our feast. Jasmine acted like a French waiter, tea towel over her shoulder, as she poured out cranberry juice for us.

'*J'aime le vin rouge,*' I said.

'Pretending has its limits,' said Will. 'Let's get real now.' He went to the drinks cabinet in the living room and came back with a bottle of Côtes du Rhône.

'*Bon, bon, bon,*' said Jasmine, clapping.

I thought they were still playacting, but Will got the corkscrew out of the cupboard.

'Will! Dad will go berserk!'

'So what's new? Dad's always going berserk,' said Will. He dug the corkscrew right in and twisted it. He poured us all a large glass. I didn't really want any but I didn't want to be left out. I sipped the red liquid and forced my food down, wondering why it wasn't working for me. I was with my two favourite people in all the world, and yet it was like being back with Marnie and Terry, the odd one out all over again.

Jasmine drained her glass and Will filled it up immediately.

'Thank you, brother Will,' she said. She started singing her own version of 'Frère Jacques', substituting Will's name.

'Come on, let's all sing in French,' she said, waving her glass in the air. The Jasmine Fairy swayed on her chest, her wings fluttering. 'We could play a game, singing in rounds.'

'Violet and I know much better games,' said Will.

'I'm sure you do,' said Jasmine, her cheeks very pink.

'OK, we'll play *La Vérité ou un Défi*,' said Will. 'Truth or Dare, *mes petites filles*.'

'No, Will. Please don't,' I begged.

'I'll play,' said Jasmine. 'What do you have to do?'

'Simply tell the truth or perform a dare,' said Will. 'And don't think you can fob me off with fibs. I always know when someone's lying, don't I, Violet?'

'That's because you're such an expert liar yourself,' I said.

'OK, Jasmine. Violet and I have already had a go before you came, so it's your turn now,' said Will. He took a gulp of his wine and then said, 'Why did you make friends with Violet?'

162

I felt sick, scared of what she might say. Jasmine sipped her own wine, considering.

'I thought she looked the most interesting person in our class. And I was right – about her, *and* her family.'

We both smiled back at her.

'Is it my turn to ask now?' Jasmine said.

'No, it's my turn again. I distort all the rules, don't I, Violet? And it's *your* turn for a question. Are you ready? Who do you like best, Jasmine or me?'

'Oh, Will. That's silly. I like you both.'

'That's not a proper answer. Come on, choose.'

'I choose *both*,' I said. 'I can distort the rules too.'

'Oh no you can't. I think you're heading for a forfeit.' Will reached for the timer. Jasmine raised her eyebrows at me, obviously not taking any of this seriously.

'Jasmine or me?' said Will, setting the timer.

'You can stop that. I'm not choosing. I'll do the dare.'

'No, Violet, pick Will. I don't mind,' said Jasmine. 'I wouldn't trust him when it comes to dares.'

'I'm renowned for the excellence of my dares,' said Will. 'So, little indecisive sister, I dare you to go up to our attic and stay for ten minutes.'

'Oh, that's easy,' said Jasmine. 'You can do that dare, can't you, Violet?'

I sat very still. I remembered Will had said he'd put a bat box outside the attic window. Maybe bats were already flapping around our attic in the warm darkness.

'I can't.'

'You have to,' said Will. 'Look, I'll give you the timer. A piddly little ten minutes! Even you can do that.'

163

'Please don't make me, Will,' I said helplessly. 'Look, OK, I'll choose between you and Jasmine.'

'Too late,' said Will. 'You've chosen the dare. Now *do* it!'

I looked appealingly at Jasmine. She was holding onto her fairy necklace, her lips pressed together.

'Jasmine?'

'It's only a *little* dare, Violet.' She looked at Will. 'I'm sure you'll think up worse ones for me.'

He gave her a strange smile but then he frowned at me. 'Go on. Here's the timer. I'll set it for you when you're on the steps. Come on, up you go.'

'But what if there are bats?'

'Then you'll be able to do a very useful little wildlife survey and see whether they have short ears and muzzles and are therefore pipistrelles, or maybe they'll have huge great ears and be placid long-eared bats, or they *could* just be as big as your head with immensely pointed teeth and be the dreaded demon dive-bombing poison bats.'

Jasmine was falling about laughing. 'He's joking, Violet!'

I gave a nervous titter.

'Come on, up the stairs.' Will held his hand out to me.

'You can do it, Violet,' said Jasmine, taking my other hand. 'We'll applaud you when you come down and then it'll be your turn to ask *us* questions. You can use your time up in the attic to think up the most amazing embarrassing questions that will make us both squirm.'

I let them lead me up the stairs and along the landing.

164

'Can't you come up with me?' I said.

'Violet, you're deliberately missing the point.'

'Well, couldn't you go and have a look in the loft first, just to check there aren't any bats?'

'You've got bats on the brain, Violet,' said Jasmine, but she squeezed my hand sympathetically. She looked up at the closed loft entrance high above us. 'How on earth are you going to get up there?'

'Open sesame,' said Will, pulling a lever.

As if by magic the trapdoor opened and a set of steps was lowered downwards. Dad fixed it up years ago so he could store all our old stuff more conveniently. Will and I were expressly forbidden to go up into the loft because the floor didn't have any proper boards laid down.

'I'll probably fall through the joists and break my neck,' I said. 'Then you'll be sorry, Will.'

'Oh, I'd be heart-broken. If I had a heart,' said Will, adjusting the timer. 'Here you are. I've set it to go off in ten minutes.'

I snatched the timer from him and started up the steps. I kept looking up at the dark rectangle above me, waiting for the bats to come flying out into my face. I wished I'd thought to tie my hair up, even though Will said that was an old wives' tale. Why should I believe anything Will said? Why could he always make me do whatever he wanted? I looked down at him.

'Will you come and rescue me if I scream?'

'Certainly. Once your ten minutes are up. Now get on with it. The timer's ticking away and you're not even up there yet. Get *in*!'

165

I took a deep breath and tentatively took two more steps upwards, poking my head up into the entrance. It was so dark I couldn't see a thing. I listened hard for the flapping of wings. I didn't *think* I could hear anything. My pulse was beating so fast there was a drumming in my ears. I took one more step, then another. I stood shakily on the last step and walked right into the loft. I stood on a narrow joist, dizzy with fear, waiting. And waiting. And waiting . . .

I put my hand out, terrified that something might be waiting too, invisible in the dark. I couldn't feel anything in front of me. I tried moving my hand sideways, sweeping it in an arc. My fingers brushed against something small and hard and familiar on the loft wall. A light switch! I flicked it on and saw the loft properly. It wasn't the bogey bat lair of my imagination, it was a perfectly ordinary dusty room stacked with suitcases and trunks and boxes, with a big water tank in the corner.

I waited for Will to shout up to me that it was cheating to have the light on. Perhaps he couldn't see from down on the landing. I stepped gingerly from one joist to the next, making my way over to a big cardboard box containing a Sylvanian Family tree house, all my old Barbie dolls, a push-along dog on wheels. I squatted precariously beside it, stroking these once-loved toys, sucked straight back to my little-girlhood.

I started searching through the other boxes. There were lots of boring things, old tea sets, spare duvets, sports things, a box of police boots, helmets and a truncheon. Then I came to a box of baby stuff. Little pink dresses, a white hand-crocheted shawl, a musical box, a white christening robe with pink smocking, little pink and white striped booties ... I put a tiny knitted bootie on either forefinger and waggled them up and down like little glove puppets.

I started searching for boxes of Will's toys, Will's baby clothes, Will's booties. I couldn't find anything. I lifted boxes, sifting through them quickly, until I got to the far corner of the loft. There was just one box left, but it was heavily taped shut. This made me more curious. I pulled and tore at it until I got it open.

It was another box of baby things, all carefully wrapped in white tissue paper tied with blue silk ribbons. I undid each bow and found tiny cornflower-blue sleeping suits, little denim rompers, a cot-sized blue and white patchwork quilt, all in pristine condition. Right at the very bottom there was a baby book of photographs. I opened it up. I saw Mum's writing on the first page.

Our darling little William.

I hugged the book to my chest. I knew I had to show it to Will. Mum and Dad obviously loved him so much, right from the day they adopted him.

Then I looked at the birth date in Mum's royal-blue italic. It was the wrong date. I didn't understand. I looked at the photographs. There was a tiny newborn baby in a hospital crib, with a peaky heart-shaped face and long tufts of black hair. He looked eerily like me. There were photos of Mum holding him. She looked so different, much younger, her eyes bright, cheeks pink, chubby and smiling. Dad had the baby in the next photo, holding his police cap comically above the baby's head, smiling at his son so proudly. There was a big studio portrait in bright colour, the baby propped up on pillows, smiling sweetly, his eyes very big and very blue.

Will's eyes are green.

I flicked through the album to the last page. There was a small, slightly out-of-focus snapshot of Mum in a hospital ward. She was holding the baby, clutching him tightly, as if she could never bear to let him go. The baby was lying very still in her arms. His eyes were shut.

Mum had written something at the bottom of the page, her writing barely legible this time. It was another date, only three months after the one at the beginning of the book. A birth date and a death date.

The timer went off. I slapped it sharply to shut it up. I waited for Will to call to me. I didn't know what to do. He needed to see the baby book himself. I decided to wait until Jasmine went home. This was private, just about Will and me, and this first little baby brother I never knew. Mum and Dad had clearly adored this little blue-eyed boy, their first born. So they'd tried to replace him with Will.

Dear C.D,
   I don't know what to write.
   Everything's changed.
   I can't believe it.
   Love from
   Violet
   XXX

From *Midnight* by Casper Dream

Making a Wish . . .

Twelve

I laid the baby book back at the very bottom of the box, folded all the little clothes back into blue-ribboned parcels, stuck the brown tape back over the cardboard and put the box back in the corner.

I edged my way carefully back to the trapdoor, trying to sort things out in my head. I felt so sad, as if there were a real little dead baby brother cradled in that box. I switched off the light and then made my way gingerly down the ladder.

There was no sign of Will and Jasmine. I stood on the landing, still clutching the timer. Hadn't they heard it go off? Where were they?

I was about to call them when I heard Jasmine murmur something. She was in Will's room. Maybe they were hiding, waiting to jump out at me. I crept along the landing towards Will's room. I pushed his door open cautiously and peeped round.

Will and Jasmine were standing in the middle of the floor. Will had his arms round Jasmine, his hands in her beautiful hair. His head was bent. Hers was tilted upwards.

They were kissing.

I stared at them. It could have been a second, a minute, an hour. Time stood still, even though the timer ticked away in my hand.

Then Will pulled away a little. 'Your fairy's digging into my chest,' he said.

Jasmine swivelled her necklace round so that the fairy dangled over her shoulder. 'Oh dear. Poor Violet,' she said.

'Poor Violet and her flipping fairies,' said Will.

Then they both laughed.

I couldn't bear it. I ran right into the room and snatched the Jasmine Fairy from her, yanking it hard over her head.

'Yes, I know, have a good laugh! Laugh at me, both of you,' I shouted, hurling the Jasmine Fairy into a corner.

I ran to my own room. Jasmine ran after me, starting to cry.

'Oh Violet, I didn't mean—'

'Yes you did. And don't worry, I know they're silly. *I'm* silly, a teenage girl fiddling around with fairies, stupid, stupid little dolls,' I screamed.

I reached up and clawed at the Rose Fairy, the Willow, the Dragonfly, the Crow, all of them, tearing them down, pulling their heads off, snapping their limbs, crumpling their wings.

Jasmine was screaming too, begging me to stop. Will came running and tried to grab hold of my hands. I whirled away from him – and the beak of the crow scratched right down his face.

'What are you playing at, Vi?' he whispered, blood starting to trickle down his cheek.

'I've stopped playing,' I said.

I grabbed my jacket, pushed past both of them, and ran downstairs. I snatched the ten pounds still on the kitchen table and then I was out the door. I was still clutching the Crow Fairy. I hung on tight to her like a talisman and started running.

I didn't know where I was going, what I was doing. I just needed to run right away. I heard Will shouting after me but I didn't look back. I don't know if they tried to follow me. They didn't have a hope of catching me. I ran as if I had my own wings beating on my back.

I didn't stop running when I got into town. I needed to get as far away as possible. A phrase echoed in my head – *clear across three counties*. I suddenly knew where I was going. I didn't need to check the address. I knew it by heart.

I asked for a child's fare at the railway station ticket office. It was £9.99. I pocketed my penny and waited for the train. It was a complicated journey, with two changes. The man in the ticket office told me twice and I repeated it as if it was a magic charm.

I didn't know what to do with myself on the different

trains and during the lonely waits at various stations. I couldn't stop thinking about Will and Jasmine. I thought back through our brief intense friendship, wondering if she'd befriended me right from the start simply because she wanted to get to know Will. And what about him? Was he really interested in Jasmine, or was all this an elaborate game to hurt me?

I felt my head was ready to burst as I thought things through, interpreting everything this way and that. It was like so many of Casper Dream's illustrations. You'd look at a picture of an ugly old witch and a group of screaming children and first you'd think she was working evil magic and threatening them so they were yelling in terror. But then you'd look again and wonder if the witch was simply a sad old woman cowering away from taunting children intent on playing tricks on her. A painting of a beautiful nymph cradling a little rabbit could also be a hungry girl with her fingers clasped tightly round the rabbit's neck, ready to strangle it for a stew. A picture of a desperate princess in the clutches of an immense scaly serpent seemed easy enough to understand, but perhaps she was entwining the serpent willingly, her head thrown back in rapture?

I thought about these pictures, imagining all my Casper Dream books, turning the pages in my head, realizing I knew every illustration off by heart.

I arrived at the final station hours later. I stood uncertainly on the platform, not knowing where to go now. I asked an old woman if she knew Paradise Street but she muttered in a foreign accent that she was a stranger.

I asked a young man and he said he'd never heard of it. I asked a group of schoolgirls, who stared at me weirdly and shook their heads, giggling. So I stalked past them all, right out of the station. There was a taxi driver waiting out the front so I asked him if he knew.

'Sure, sweetheart. Hop in,' he said.

'No, I don't want a taxi ride,' I said, blushing. 'I want to walk. Could you possibly tell me the way?'

He sighed and then rattled off a long list of complicated directions, left, left, right, right again until my head was spinning.

'Are you taking this in?' he said.

I nodded, not daring to ask him to repeat it again.

'Rubbish, you haven't a clue, have you?' he said. 'Go on, jump in the cab. I'll take you.'

'But I haven't got any money.'

'Never mind. I can't have you blundering around all over the town. And Paradise Road isn't in a very nice area.'

'It's very kind of you.'

'I've got a daughter your age, darling. I like to think another cabbie would help her out the same way.'

He gave me a lift through many murky streets, skirting blackened warehouses and tough council estates and rows of boarded-up shops, turning down identical bleak streets of tumbledown terraced houses to Paradise Street. It was an ugly street of squat pebbledashed houses with unkempt gardens and rubbish strewn along the gutters.

175

'Are you *sure* you want Paradise Street?' said the taxi driver.

'Yes please. Number twenty-eight,' I said.

The taxi driver drew up outside the right house. The pebbledash had fallen off the walls here and there, and some of the roof tiles were missing. Someone had tacked polythene up at the windows as crude double glazing, making the house look bleary-eyed. The front door was a harsh pillar-box red, like a gash of bright lipstick on a faded old woman.

It *couldn't* be the right house. Someone as artistic as Casper Dream could never have lived here. But I didn't have anywhere else to go, so I thanked the taxi driver fervently for the free lift and pretended everything was fine. He sat in his cab and watched me, looking doubtful. I couldn't possibly hover on the pavement. I had to let myself in the broken gate and walk up the pathway. I waited when I got to the garish front door. I knocked – and the taxi driver finally drove away.

I waited a couple of seconds, holding my breath, and then darted back down the pathway to the gate. I wasn't quite quick enough. Before I could unlatch it the front door opened.

'Hey, what do you want?'

It was a youngish woman with a tired white face, a grizzling baby drooping on her hip.

'Oh! I'm sorry. I think I've come to the wrong house,' I gabbled.

'Oh yeah?' she said suspiciously, looking me up and down. 'Who did you want to see?'

I took a deep breath. 'Well, I think Casper Dream might have lived here once,' I said.

'You what? Some bloke called *Casper* lived here? I doubt that very much.'

'Have you lived here a while then?'

'Only six months, and that's long enough. It's a disgrace, this dump. I've been backwards and forwards to the council ever since the baby was born but they won't listen. He's chesty already – he'll get asthma if we don't get out soon.'

The baby started crying harder as if he understood. She joggled him on her hip. 'I'd better feed him. Well, off you go then.'

'Yes. Sorry. Goodbye,' I said, as she closed the door.

I edged round the gate and stood staring at her house. I *must* have remembered it wrong. But I'd known it by heart for years, as well as I knew my own address. Still, what did it really matter? Casper Dream certainly wasn't here now.

I closed my eyes tight, scared I was going to start crying right there in the street. I put my hands inside my jacket pockets, clasping the Crow Fairy tight. I heard footsteps. I opened my eyes and saw a very fat man lumbering along the pavement towards me. He was so huge he had to waddle. When he got nearer I could hear the wheeze of his breath.

I liked the way he looked, even though his vast bulk was grotesque. He was wearing a huge olive-velvet jacket, gigantic black jeans and purple suede boots. His longish fair hair kept falling forward across his face. He was pink with the effort of walking. I didn't like to keep staring at him. He must be so sick of people peering. I swivelled my eyes back to the house and stared at the front door instead.

I waited for the fat man to walk past. He was walking very slowly now, his purple boots barely moving. Then he stopped altogether, almost beside me. He breathed rapidly, wheezing a little. I could smell his lemon cologne. He reached in his jacket pocket, found a silk handkerchief and mopped his brow. Then he gave me a quick shy nod and started shuffling off, back the way he had come.

Perhaps he'd made a special pilgrimage to Number 28 Paradise Street too. There could only be one reason why.

'Excuse me,' I called timidly after his large back. 'I know this sounds silly, but do you like Casper Dream?'

He stopped. He turned round, looking wary. 'Why did you ask that?' he said.

'Because I think he once lived here. And you seemed to be looking at the house too.'

'Do *you* like Casper Dream?' he said.

'I love him. I've got all his books, even *The Smoky Fairy*. I know them off by heart, all twelve.'

'Which do you like the most?'

'I think ... Well, I like them all, but maybe I like *Midnight* most.'

'Which page?'

'The last one, where the princess is looking out of her palace window. Well, I *think* it's a palace – I suppose it could also be a prison, it's hard to tell in the moonlight.

There's a church with a steeple in the distance and the clock is striking midnight. It says on the page opposite the picture that if you wish between the chimes of one and twelve then your wish will come true.'

'Does it say that? Doesn't it say *maybe* your wish will come true?'

'Yes, it does! So you really are a fan if you know the books so well.'

Surprisingly, he shook his head. 'No, I wouldn't call myself a fan. I could find fault with every single illustration.'

'But they're beautiful! Each and every one of them, even when he's drawing ugly or evil things. They're the most wonderful illustrations ever!' I said indignantly.

'Well, I shan't argue with you. I'm sure Casper Dream would be very proud if he knew there was such an ardent supporter of his work.'

'I've always said I'm his number one fan, only that's ridiculous, because hundreds and thousands of people love his books. There's a fan club too, but it's just run by his publishers. He doesn't contribute to the website himself.'

'I've heard he's very elusive,' said the fat man.

'No one knows where he lives and he never gives interviews and he won't do book signings and he doesn't write to anyone.'

'No one at all?'

'Well, perhaps he did once, long ago,' I said, hugging my secret to myself. I couldn't help smiling and the fat man smiled back.

'Did he write to you once too?' I asked. 'Is that how you know about this house?'

'I've always known about this house,' he said.

I looked at him very carefully. I stared at his face and imagined it in shadow, at an angle.

'It's you!' I whispered.

'And I think I know you too. You're . . . it's a flowery name. Wait a minute. It's Violet!'

'How do you know me?'

'You really are my number one fan, Violet. You were the first person to write to me about my books. I treasured your letter.'

'And you wrote back to me with your address. I wrote back again, but that letter came back unopened.'

'I moved away. And then when the next book got published I was deluged with letters. I decided I couldn't write back any more. I'm sorry.'

'I understand. I still write to you though.'

'What, to my publishers?'

'No, I write a letter and then I put it in a big silver box at the back of my wardrobe. It's like I'm pretending to post it.'

'That's a lovely idea. But I don't suppose you'll want to write any more letters now you know what I'm really like. I'm not exactly a handsome prince, am I?'

'I think you *are* handsome. Quite,' I said.

'You're a very kind girl, Violet.' He fumbled in his pocket again and found a little leather notepad and a pen.

'Are you going to give me an autograph?'

'If you'd like one. And a little picture?'

'Please!'

He rested the notepad in his left hand and started drawing. I watched carefully as the black lines arranged themselves on the page into a familiar small fairy, looking down, head slightly on one side.

'It's the Violet Fairy!'

'It is indeed.'

'It's magic watching her appear just like that on the page. I feel as if *this* is magic. I mean, I didn't even know I was coming here this morning. I live miles and miles away. But now I'm here and you're here too, by the most amazing, wonderful coincidence.'

'It's not quite such a coincidence. I come here most days. I have a chauffeur waiting round the corner. I take my little constitutional along this road as far as the house. I pause for a minute or two and while I'm catching my breath I remember a time when I wasn't Casper Dream.'

'So who were you?'

'This is a secret, Violet.'

'I won't tell anyone, you know I won't.'

'I was a sad shy fat boy called Colin Dunwell. I wasn't very happy at home – *this* home – and I hated school. I wasn't very clever, so that everyone used to say, "Hasn't he Dunwell," as a sarcastic joke.'

'You must have been good at art.'

'I suppose I was, but no one took art seriously. And I didn't draw the sort of things I liked to draw, not at school. But at home I shut myself up in my room and drew

181

my own fairy world – though I had to hide all my drawings from my brothers or they'd have teased me mercilessly. I hoped to go to art college but I had to leave school at sixteen to go and work in my uncle's newsagent's shop. I hated that too. I'm not very good at meeting people – and all that chocolate was much too tempting too. I ate all day and half the night. I still do, though Olivia keeps gently nagging me to lose some of the weight. She's my editor and now she's my partner too.'

'With long blonde hair,' I said, sighing.

'That's right. You know so much about me, Violet. I sent her *The Smoky Fairy*. I wrote it in my teens, while I was still working at the newsagent's. I sent it to so many publishers and they all turned it down. This went on for years. I got so depressed. I felt I'd never ever achieve my dream, but then Olivia saw the manuscript, liked the artwork, asked if we could meet ... And later, when there was all the fuss and the book had to be withdrawn she still had enough faith in me to commission a new book. Now my whole life's changed and I still can't quite believe it. I don't want to be part of the whole arty literary scene. I'd hate that. And I don't look the part, obviously. So I don't want fame – and I'm not that fussed about the fortune either, though it's lovely to live in a house I like and I can fill it with beautiful things. But the most magical thing of all is being able to work all day creating my own fairy worlds.

'I like to come here and remember just for a minute what it was like before. I'm so grateful now that I lived in this ugly house and was always the odd one out because that made me invent my own world of tiny beautiful beings. There we are, here's your fairy.'

He'd drawn the Violet Fairy so beautifully, adding long dark hair just like mine.

To Violet, my number one fan.
I'm so glad we met.
Make a wish at midnight!

With all good wishes from Casper Dream

'I shall make a wish,' I said.

'Do you like art too?'

'Yes, but I don't really draw much. I sew.'

'What do you sew?'

I took a deep breath. 'I sew fairies. Your fairies.' I scrabbled in my pocket and brought out the torn Crow Fairy.

'Oh my goodness, she's wonderful! She's exactly

right. There are some Casper Dream fairy doll things but I hate them.'

'I hate them too. You can have the Crow Fairy if you like, though her leg's coming off – and some of her hair's missing. I got mad about something and tore down all my fairies.'

'I would like the Crow Fairy very much. She's exquisite. But do you know what I think you should do, Violet? I think you should invent your own creatures. You're so skilled. Create your own dreamworld. I wanted a very small world because I'm so big. You're so small, maybe you might want to create large things. Think big and beautiful!'

I thought about it all the way home. Casper Dream had his chauffeur drive me to the railway station. I negotiated my way home again, making all the train changes, tucking my picture of the Violet Fairy very carefully into my pocket so that it wouldn't get crumpled.

Then I walked home from the station. Dad's car wasn't in the driveway so at least I was back before them. I felt sick at the thought of seeing Will. What would I do if Jasmine was still there? I had to knock at the door because I didn't have my key.

Will opened it – and then he put his arms round me and hugged me hard.

'I thought you'd never come back. I didn't know what to do. I even thought about phoning Mum and Dad. I was so *worried*. I thought you'd be back in a few minutes. So did Jasmine. She waited for hours but then she had to go home. She feels terrible. She thinks it's all her fault. But it's my fault, I know. It's always my fault. I don't know why I'm so mean to you. Something just makes me. Maybe the old granny bat is right, it's bad blood.'

'That's rubbish,' I said, hugging him back. 'Look, I know why Mum and Dad have always been so weird with you, why they sometimes act like you're the wrong boy, the changeling. There was another William once, their first baby. He died when he was little. They shouldn't have adopted you – it wasn't fair, trying to replace him like that, but I'm so glad they did because you're my brother now.'

'How do you know all this stuff?' Will asked, still holding me.

'Come up to the loft and I'll show you.'

We climbed up there and looked at the baby things together. Will was silent when he saw the photos.

'I wonder if I looked like him when I was a baby? Maybe the dark hair?' Will peered at the last photo of the little dead baby and shuddered. 'Let's put all these baby things back in the box.'

'It's awful, it's like poor little baby Will's coffin.'

'Maybe we'll find a little blue pot of his ashes somewhere?'

'Shut *up*, Will!'

But we were fine together in the attic. It only started to get awkward when we came down the stairs. We both glanced involuntarily along the landing to Will's bedroom.

'So is Jasmine your girlfriend now?' I asked.

185

'I – I don't know. She wants to be *your* friend. Come on, give her a ring to let her know you're back safely.'

'I don't want to.'

'Violet, she's desperately worried.'

'Then you ring her.'

Will dialled the number, but then he held the phone out to me, pressing it against my ear.

'Hello? Violet? Is that you? Oh please, please let it be you!' Jasmine said, her voice thick, as if she was crying.

'It's me,' I whispered.

'Are you all right? Are you back home? Oh Violet, please say we're still friends.'

'You don't really want to be my friend. You just wanted to get to know Will,' I said.

'That's not true. Well, I *did* want to get to know Will, but I wanted to be your friend before that. Don't you remember? In the classroom, that first day? I practically begged you to be my friend and I didn't even know you had a brother then.'

I thought back.

'I'm right, aren't I?' Jasmine persisted. 'I wanted you to be my friend because you looked so different from the others, and you were so sweet to me, and we just kind of clicked, as if we'd known each other for always. And now I've mucked it all up, haven't I?'

I took a deep breath. 'No you haven't. We're still friends,' I said.

'Best friends?'

'Best friends, no matter what,' I said, and then I put the phone down.

Will had gone into the kitchen and was wolfing down the remains of the picnic. I stuffed cheese and prawns and bread and grapes into my mouth too, suddenly ravenous.

When we'd eaten every morsel and were feeling so stuffed we couldn't move we heard the car draw up outside. Mum and Dad came in, looking pink and windswept. They'd walked for miles along the seafront after visiting Gran. Mum was lugging a huge carrier of Chinese takeaway food.

'I felt so bad about leaving you two without a proper cooked meal,' she said.

'I told you they'd be fine,' said Dad. 'You *are* fine, aren't you, you awkward little tykes?' He looked at us both. 'Look, those things I said. Forget it. I got a bit worked up. We'll let bygones be bygones. Come on, let's all start noshing.'

Will managed a plateful but I couldn't eat more than a mouthful.

'There's seaweed and prawns, your favourites, Violet. Why aren't you eating?' said Mum. 'Is there something wrong, dear?'

'Well . . .' I hesitated. And then I couldn't stop myself. 'Yes, there *is* something wrong. I was looking in the attic for something—'

'Don't!' said Will.

'You're not allowed in the attic, you know that,' Dad said.

'Yes, but the thing is, I found . . . I found all the stuff about baby Will.'

187

Mum and Dad stopped eating. It was just like magic, as if I'd turned them into statues. Their hands were holding their knives and forks, their mouths were open. Will rocked on his chair, his face screwed up.

'Shut up, Violet,' he muttered.

'No. We've all shut up for far too long. Why can't we talk about him?'

'Because it'll upset your mother,' said Dad furiously, throwing his cutlery down on his plate with a clatter.

Mum shook her head, as if she was coming out of a trance. 'It's all right,' she said softly, although tears started rolling down her cheeks. 'We should have told you, I know we should. I just couldn't bear to think back to when he died. It was my fault—'

'Of course it wasn't your fault! It was a cot death,' said Dad, and he reached out and took Mum's hand. 'You *know* that.'

'I should have stayed up watching over him. He wasn't well—'

'He had a little cold, that's all. And we had his baby alarm on, so we could hear his little snuffles,' said Dad.

'But when we woke up we couldn't hear anything,' Mum said, weeping.

'And when we went to look, we knew he was gone, we knew straight away, even though I tried to give him the kiss of life, poor little lamb,' said Dad, and there were tears in his eyes too. He was looking at me, explaining. 'And then we went through such a bad time, and I was off work with compassionate leave, and then the very day I went back, almost as if it was fate, I was involved in this sad case – young mum, drug overdose, little baby going through withdrawals. We went to see the baby – and it was the weirdest thing, he had blue eyes and a mop of black curls, just like our William. So we had to have him, even though it took months of paperwork and his health was pretty dodgy for a while. But eventually we got him and he was ours.'

'Will's eyes are green,' I said.

'All babies have blue eyes at first. But then they change,' said Mum, wiping her cheeks with the back of her free hand.

'I changed all right,' said Will.

'I'm so sorry we didn't tell you sooner,' said Mum, looking at him. 'I just wanted to pretend but it was so wrong of me not to tell you about our first little Will.'

'I'm the second,' said Will. 'Second best,' he added bitterly.

Mum stood up, letting go of Dad. She went round the table to Will, putting her hands on his shoulders. He tried to duck away from her but she hung on tightly.

'You come first now,' she said. 'You're still our boy, no matter what. Isn't he?' She was looking over at Dad now.

He missed a couple of beats, maybe making it plain what he really felt. Or maybe he was simply too tense and embarrassed to react at first. But after a few seconds he suddenly nodded.

'Of course you're our son,' he said.

I clasped my hands tight in my lap and prayed that Will wouldn't say the wrong thing. In the end he didn't say anything at all. He just nodded and then walked slowly out of the room.

'Should I go after him?' said Mum.

'No, leave the lad alone for now,' said Dad.

I wanted to be on my own too. I went up to my room, saying I had to get some homework finished. I looked up at my ceiling. The fairies weren't there any more. There was no trace of them, not a wing, a limb, a lock of hair. It was as if they'd simply flown away.

I got out all my materials and started sifting them around. I sketched a few outlines on the back of an envelope. Then I took a large piece of brown paper for a pattern. I drew baby shapes on it, small at first, but then I turned the paper over and drew bigger, bolder, fashioning my own pattern, a lifesize newborn baby.

I cut it out and started looking for the right material for the skin. Not pink, not white. I had a pale-green silky shirt. It would make perfect flesh for a fairy changeling.

I worked hard all evening, pinning, cutting and sewing. I couldn't find my favourite needle and some of my thread seemed to have gone missing, but I made do as best I could.

Mum came knocking on my door to say goodnight.

'Don't come in, Mum, I'm working on a secret,' I said.

'That's funny. I've just said goodnight outside Will's door and he says *he's* working on something. You're a strange pair,' said Mum. 'What on earth did you get up to all day? I was worried about you.'

'We were fine, Mum, honestly. Goodnight.'

'Don't keep that light on too long, will you?' Dad

called. ' 'Night, Violet. 'Night, Will.'

I called goodnight back. I couldn't hear whether Will did or not. I put my main light out but went on working by my bedside lamp, wanting my baby to start taking shape. The house was still and silent. I watched the clock, waiting for midnight. Then I heard Will creeping across the landing, sliding a note under my door. I opened it up.

Look out of your window in ten minutes. Will.

I heard the faint scrape of the back door opening downstairs. Will was going out into the garden. I wondered what he was doing, but decided to wait the ten minutes so as not to spoil his surprise.

I sewed my baby's face, choosing eyes as green as grass with long black lashes. Then I went to the window and looked out. Our own garden was in darkness but there was an eerie light next door in the wilderness. I saw a dark shadow. It was Will with a torch, lighting up Miss Lang's old apple tree.

I leaned forward, my head against the cold glass. The branches were bearing strange fruit. I opened my window and leaned right out into the night. It wasn't fruit – it was fairies. Will had stitched my poor torn fairies back together. There they were, hanging from the tree by threads, spinning in the wind.

Will moved the torch, showing me all of them. A bat flew in the golden light above his head, then another, and another, like flying goblins. I heard a clock chime far away. It was striking midnight.

I looked out into the night and made my wish.

Dear Violet,
   I very much enjoyed meeting you the other day. I think I owe
you a letter! It means so much to me that you like my work,
and know it so well! I shall send you an early copy of the thir-
teenth book. I think I shall call it Magical Encounters. It's
going to be dedicated to somebody special . . .
   With very best wishes
   Casper Dream

ABOUT THE AUTHOR

JACQUELINE WILSON was born in Bath in 1945, but has spent most of her life in Kingston-on-Thames, Surrey. She always wanted to be a writer and wrote her first 'novel' when she was nine, filling countless Woolworths' exercise books as she grew up. She started work at a publishing company and then went on to work as a journalist on *Jackie* magazine (which was named after her) before turning to writing fiction full-time.

Since 1990 Jacqueline has written prolifically for children and has won many of the UK's top awards for children's books, including the Guardian Children's Fiction Award, the Smarties Prize and the Children's Book of the Year. Jacqueline was awarded an OBE in the Queen's Birthday Honours list, in Goldeen Jubilee Year, 2002.

Over 15 million copies of Jacqueline's books have now been sold in the UK and approximately 50,000 copies of her books are sold each month. An avid reader herself, Jacqueline has a personal collection of more than 15,000 books.

She has one grown-up daughter.

ABOUT THE ILLUSTRATOR

NICK SHARRATT knew from an early age that he wanted to use his artistic skills in his career. He went to Manchester Polytechnic to do an Art Foundation course, followed by a BA (Hons) in Graphic Design at St Martin's School of Art in London. Since graduating in 1984, Nick has been working full-time as an illustrator, with his work much in demand for magazines and children's books. He has also designed and illustrated packaging for confectionery.

His famous collaboration with Jacqueline Wilson began with *The Story of Tracy Beaker*, published in 1991 and he has illustrated every one of her best-selling books published by Doubleday / Corgi since then.

Nick also illustrates full-colour picture and novelty books, such as *Eat Your Peas* (Bodley Head), written by Kes Gray, which won the 2000 Children's Book Award. He also writes his own books, including *The Cheese and Tomato Spider* (Scholastic) which won the 1997 Sheffield Children's Book Award.

After living in London for thirteen years, Nick moved to Gloucestershire and then to Brighton, Sussex, where he now lives. When he is not working, he loves to eat – he says that food is a major part of his life!

THE DIAMOND GIRLS

Jacqueline Wilson

'You're all *my favourite Diamond girls,'* said Mum.
'Little sparkling gems, the lot of you . . .'

Dixie, Rochelle, Jude and Martine – the Diamond girls!
They might sound like a girl band but these sisters' lives
are anything but glamorous. They've moved into a
terrible house on a run-down estate and after barely five
minutes Rochelle's flirting, Jude's fighting and Martine's
storming off. Even though Dixie's the youngest, she's
desperate to get the house fixed up before Mum comes
home – with her new baby! Will the Diamond girls pull
together in time for the first Diamond boy?

A typical slice of real life – tough on the outside,
warm on the inside – from the bestselling,
multi-award-winning Jacqueline Wilson.

Now available in Doubleday hardcover

0 385 60607 9

BEST FRIENDS

Jacqueline Wilson

*Alice is my very best friend. I don't
know what I'd do without her.*

Gemma and Alice have been best friends since they
were born. They see each other every day. It never
seems to matter that Gemma loves football while Alice
prefers drawing or that Gemma never stops talking
while Alice is more likely to be listening. They share
everything. Then one day Gemma finds out that
there's something Alice isn't sharing. A Secret. And
when Gemma finally discovers what it is, she isn't
sure if she and Alice can stay Best Friends Forever . . .

A delightfully touching and entertaining story
from a best-selling, prize-winning author.

Now available in Doubleday hardcover

0 385 60606 0

SECRETS

Jacqueline Wilson

'I keep a diary,' Treasure said.'
I keep a diary, too,' said India, and then she blushed.

Treasure and India are two girls with very different
backgrounds. As an unlikely but deep friendship
develops between them, they keep diaries, inspired by
their heroine, Anne Frank. Soon the pages are filled
with the details of their most serious secret ever . . .

A superbly moving novel for older readers from
the prize-winning author of *The Illustrated Mum*
and *The Story of Tracy Beaker*.

'The Diary of Anne Frank is woven into this story . . .
this could have been a dangerous device for a
lesser novelist; Wilson carries it off triumphantly.
This brilliant writer still provides her fans with
reality at its most unvarnished' *Independent*

'Wilson's skilful way with dialogue and plot
makes this a moving, funny and uplifting
story about friendship' *Observer*

Corgi Yearling Books

0 440 86508 5

THE ILLUSTRATED MUM

Jacqueline Wilson

*Star used to love Marigold, love me, love our life
together. We three were the colourful ones,
like the glowing pictures inked all over Marigold . . .*

Covered from head to foot with glorious tattoos,
Marigold is the brightest, most beautiful mother in
the world. That's what Dolphin thinks (she just
wishes her beautiful mum wouldn't stay out partying
all night or go weird now and then). Her older sister,
Star, isn't so sure any more. She loves Marigold too,
but sometimes she just can't help wishing she
were more normal . . .

A powerful and memorable tale for older readers
from Jacqueline Wilson, the award-winning
author of *The Suitcase Kid*, *Double Act*,
Bad Girls and many other titles.

WINNER OF THE 2000 BRITISH BOOK AWARD (NIBBIES)
WINNER OF THE CHILDREN'S BOOK OF THE YEAR AWARD
WINNER OF THE GUARDIAN CHILDREN'S FICTION AWARD
HIGHLY COMMENDED FOR THE CARNEGIE MEDAL

Corgi Yearling Books

0 440 86368 6

BAD GIRLS

Jacqueline Wilson

Kim's gang had better watch out! Because Tanya's my friend now, and she'll show them

Mandy has been picked on at school for as long as she can remember. That's why she is delighted when cheeky, daring, full-of-fun Tanya picks her as a friend. Mum isn't happy – she thinks Tanya's a BAD GIRL and a bad influence. Mandy's sure Tanya can only get her out of trouble, not in to it . . . or could she?

SHORTLISTED FOR THE CARNEGIE MEDAL

Corgi Yearling Books

0 440 86356 2

For all the latest news, information and events and to join the official Jacqueline Wilson Fan Club, log on to

www.jacquelinewilson.co.uk